A Swirl of Colors and Jagged Edges

Angela L Keith

A Swirl of Colors and Jagged Edges

ISBN 979-8-9925233-1-7 Print

ISBN 979-8-9925233-0-0 Ebook

Dedicated to my half-pint hooligans, DMK and DJK

Chapter One

RAFE'S coffee is bitter. It tastes like he shook the beans in a pan under a blazing fire to a crisp, before grinding and brewing. I don't know anything really about the business of coffee, but his tastes bad and Mom's coffee always tasted amazing. She bought her beans from the Co-Op and used the French press. Each cup produced something smooth, slightly smokey with a hint of chocolate. It's not his fault. He's doing the best he can, given the circumstances.

He sits across from me at our small kitchen table gripping his cup with both hands, bringing it to rest just below his lips before setting it down again, never once taking a drink. I take another sip from my own, fighting the urge to cringe.

"It's okay to admit you don't like it," he says, smiling. It's a gentle, boyish grin, the left side of his mouth pulling up slightly higher than the right.

"It's not that bad."

"Really? Why don't you take a real drink then, without spewing, and tell me it's not that bad."

"Alright fine." I shove the mug away. "The coffee sucks."

"Your mom was the coffee connoisseur in this house. Guess I should have paid more attention to how she brewed it. Instant coffee mix is apparently not the same."

"You could have just gone to Roasters, you know," I say.

He nods. "Not today. We'll just have to talk without the coffee." He gets up, takes our mugs to the sink and rinses them out. When he returns, he pulls a manila envelope from his messenger bag, slides it across the table. I receive it, resting my hand on top, allowing for my fingers to trace the swirly letters of my name, in her handwriting.

"We don't have to do this now," Rafe says. "I know today will be especially difficult, but she wanted me to make sure you got this before you left in the fall."

I close my eyes and nod, hand still resting on the envelope. "We can do it now," I croak. I'm trying so hard to keep my shit together, and I know it's ridiculous because in a matter of hours, three to be exact, we'll pull up to the funeral home, take our place in the first row of seats, and listen as people pay their respects to my mother's cremated remains. Everything after that will just be a blur, I'm sure of it. So yeah, Rafe. Let's have this conversation now.

I slide my index finger under the sealed flap and gently pry it open, tugging out a stack of documents. Deed to the bungalow. Title to her car. Lease papers on the studio. And lastly, a handwritten letter. My mother loved to hand-write letters. Thank you notes to the mail carrier; words of encouragement scribbled on post-It's left in my lunch boxes; on the steering wheel of my car; on my bathroom mirror. I'm not surprised at all to find this letter, scribbled some time in her last days when she could still hold a pen.

I'm not ready to read it yet so I fold it and tuck it into the pocket of my cardigan. Some things take time. Rafe stares at me, waiting for me to respond to the contents of the envelope, but here's the thing. I don't know what I'm supposed to say. Mom left me the house? Cool, I've always wanted to own a tiny, high-maintenance bungalow at eighteen. *NOT*. Lease to the yoga studio? What the heck am I supposed to do with a yoga studio? Thanks Mom, but yoga was always your thing. I'd rather just have you back, if it's all the same.

When she was first diagnosed with stage four breast cancer at the beginning of my senior year of high school, Mom took it in stride. Didn't get overly emotional, didn't curse the powers that be, or tell the doctors to run the tests again. She didn't even ask for a second opinion, which if you ask me is just stupid. Always get a second opinion. Instead, she asked how long (six months, eight if she's lucky since it had metastasized) went home, lit some incense, fumbled around with some crystals, and then asked if we wanted roman-style chicken for dinner or Mexican take-out.

She didn't like to talk about her illness. She never got mad if anyone asked her about it, she just didn't openly bring it up. She said she didn't want the special treatment. Ok, fine, whatever, the only problem was, Ashland is a small enough town, and she ran the only yoga studio. Half the town are aging hippies who take yoga. She may not have wanted the special treatment, but everyone wanted to give it to her anyway.

Her first few months after the diagnosis were jam-packed with doctor visits, trips to Portland, long arduous chemo sessions that left her so wiped out she didn't even want to practice yoga, like at all. After the first round, when it didn't seem things were getting any better, Mom decided to stop all treatment and enjoy the short amount of time she had left. Of course, my first response was that of a petulant teenager.

"Mom you've only done one round of chemo and you're already giving up? That's bull-shit!" I cried.

"Maddie, honey I'm not giving up," she said, reaching for her magenta wig and straightening it onto her head.

"Oh really? What do you call it then?"

"I call it letting the universe take over. Honey, I'm going one way or another. One round of chemo, or forty, I'm going, and I'm at peace with that." I started to protest but she put up a hand to stop me.

"When I go, I want to go out being me, not some drugged up version of me."

"But what about graduation?" I said between heaping sobs. "Without the chemo you won't make it."

She wiped my cheeks with her scarf and gripped my shoulders, turning me to face her. With her eyes that matched mine perfectly she said, "Nothing will keep me from watching you walk across that stage. I promise."

Her determination and pure stubbornness saw her through the rest of my school year until graduation. There were tears, angry outburst (mostly from me) and a shit ton of bargaining (also mostly from me), but the day of graduation, when my name was called and I walked across the stage to receive my diploma, she was there, front and center in a bedazzled wheelchair and a fuchsia wig, ginormous smile spread across a boney face. Two weeks later, in her bright canary yellow bedroom, with Rafe and myself on either side of her, she died. On her terms.

"Maddie?" Rafe says, tapping on the envelope, bringing my attention back to the topic at hand. "You sure you don't want to wait until after the service?"

"No, we can do this now. Um, was there anything in particular you needed to say? I mean, I don't even know what to do with any of this stuff."

"Well, she left the house and car to you. We'll be meeting with Mr. Broesder to go over the final documents and her Will. I uh, well I can find an apartment if you'll give me time."

I look up at him, completely shocked. What did he mean, *find an apartment*? Technically Rafe isn't my stepdad, but he's been this major figure in my life since I was five. When I was two, my dad, William Crawley decided he didn't have what it takes to parent a child. Apparently, my unplanned presence got in the way of his leading actor status with the touring Shakespeare Festival. He left on tour for King Lear and didn't come back for two years. Once he returned, I only saw him when it was convenient for him.

Mom was pretty bummed but then she met Rafe. He'd opened up an art studio in the space next to her yoga studio. A few friendly smiles and one complementary yoga session later, she was hooked. I mean, I couldn't blame her. As far as older dudes go, Rafe is a good-looking dude. Six feet, dark chocolate eyes, a thick mop of salt and pepper hair, light Spanish accent. Anyway, they just connected in a way that she's never connected with anyone, not even my father, and he wasn't intimidated at all by her lifestyle. In fact, he seemed to embrace it. Before long he was joining us for our floor dinners, yoga retreats, and trips to the Oregon Country fair. He also fell right into the role of stand-in dad, taking me to school, going to sporting events, "Daddy-Daughter" dances when my own dad was too busy to show up. Pretty soon I just thought of him as my actual dad, and my biological dad as some dude I have dinner with once a month. I couldn't imagine a life without Rafe, even with my mom gone, *especially* with her being gone.

"Wait what do you mean? Are you leaving?" I ask.

"Well honey, your mom and I were never married, I'm not your father and now that she's gone..."

"You'll what?" I interject, chest beginning to heave, "you'll leave me too?"

He reaches his hands across the table and takes hold of mine. "Maddie, honey, you have to know that I would never want to leave you. I love you so much, as if you were my own flesh and blood daughter. Your mom was my soul and you, my heart. With us not being related, I wasn't sure if, well if you'd want to stay with me. I know you're going to college, but you'll still need a home to come back to, and of course I want to be that home."

I squeeze his hands and smile. "Don't go. I need you."

Before anything else can be said, the kitchen door bursts open and a 5'11 blonde bombshell otherwise known as my best friend Erin Whitney stumbles in.

"Crap! You guys were in the middle of something. I can come back!" She turns to leave but I grab her hand.

"Come back and sit down, you Amazon," I say.

"OMG for the last time, my family is Norwegian." Erin sits down next to me, sweeps her long hair across her shoulder and weaves it effortlessly into a braid. If there was ever someone to be jealous of, it would be Erin. With her long legs, slender elfin frame and Targaryen-blonde hair she was the total package. But don't ever tell her that because she hates when people compliment her on her looks (she's also wicked smart, cusses like a sailor, and has the temper to match).

"So," Erin says, popping one of Rafe's famous broccoli-cheese quiche bites into her mouth, "I checked with the priest guy,"

"Not a priest," I interject.

"Whatever," she continues. "He's gonna have everything ready at the funeral home and Lenny's handled the programs. I've got a dope funeral playlist all queued up on my phone, so whenever you guys are ready, we can roll."

"What the heck is a funeral playlist?" I ask.

"It's mostly just a bunch of emo songs about death and dying and such but it's cool. You'll love it."

"Well, guess the only thing to do now is get this over with. Rafe, you ready?" It's a dumb question. Is anyone ever ready to go bury their loved ones? A resounding NOPE.

***

I'm standing next to a table decked out with photos of my mom; a poster-board collage capturing all the best moments of her life in Ashland. People have been coming over, paying their respects, lingering over the photos, dropping donations into an envelope and signing a memory book. Rafe thought it would be nice to have people jot down their best memory of Mom. It's totally stupid because duh, she's not ever going to see it, but he tells me it's more for them than for her. Just another way for them to truly say their last goodbyes. I shake hands and hug until I'm pretty sure I don't ever want to be touched again. How is it possible to keep a smile plastered across the face for so long?

Most of the service is a blur. The funeral director says some words, followed by a few friends from Wellsprings where Mom often taught yoga sessions during retreats and events, and then it's my turn to say something and that goes about as well as a wet fart. People expect me to give some grandly amazing eulogy, probably because I was part of the monologue team at school (yup that's a thing) but as I stand at the make-shift pulpit, with all those sad eyes blinking up at me, it's like I've forgotten the basics of language. Instead, I mutter a few unintelligible words until Rafe swoops in, wraps an arm around my shoulders and says what I can't. While he's talking, my eyes connect with those belonging to a woman I've never seen before and for a moment I think I'm seeing a ghost because though she's somewhere near the age of 70 with a petite frame and a mop of grey hair weaved into a braided bun on the top of her head, she bears an uncanny resemblance to my mother.

When the service concludes, we gather up the poster board, the flower arrangements, and the rose gold Urn that holds the contents of my mother, and head down to Pioneer Hall for a small intimate reception. Had it been up to me I'd have skipped this part all together, but Rafe thinks it would be nice for those closest to her to be able to gather one last time and celebrate her life. After more handshakes and hugs (gah!) I park myself in front of a bowl of chips while the usual group starts up one final drum circle. Erin sidles up next to me, plucking a chip from the bowl and dredging it through salsa.

"You doing okay?" she asks, wiping salsa juice from her chin with the sleeve of her sweater.

"All things considered," I reply. "Where's Leonard?"

Erin points to the corner of the room where Leonard is engaged in a heated conversation with the dude who owns the one and only bookstore in town. "Lenny found out Mr. Jones recently published a book on black holes so they're having some discussion on general relativity."

"Well that sounds like a major snooze fest," I say. Anything having to do with science is really not my cup of tea. Ask me to conjugate verbs in foreign languages or recite *Beowulf* in its entirety, no prob, but ask me to figure out genotypes using a Punnett square, well, forget about it. When Leonard was in utero, his mom's water broke at the Science Works Museum. Two seconds later he came sloshing out at the doors of the planetarium, which he credits as the catalyst to his love of all thing's science.

"Lenny thinks Mr. Jones missed some very crucial data and of course Mr. Jones disagrees because you know, he's middle aged and Lenny's just a kid so he can't possibly think he knows more. I told him a funeral reception really isn't the best place to discuss this but you know how he gets when he's debating science." She pops another chip into her mouth. "I'm gonna go redirect him."

She leaves in a whir and I head to the buffet to load up a plate with some food before returning to my seat behind the drum circle. Half way through eating something resembling a frittata, the elderly woman I saw at the service weaves her way through a group and stops in front of me.

"Hello, child. Is this seat taken?" She motions to the seat next to me with her boney fingers. I shake my head and wipe my mouth with a napkin.

"Nope. It's all yours."

She smiles and nods, gathering up her long turquoise skirt and sitting down. She's probably going to start making small talk, which I hate. But I guess I'll do it because if I don't Rafe will give me the what-for.

"Such a lovely service," she says. Her voice is soft with the faintest hint of an accent I can't quite place.

"Thank you. Of course, my mother would have been happy to have just had a few friends over to send her off, but she knew a lot of people so hence the service."

"I think she would have loved it," the old woman says, her voice cracking.

I cock my head to the side and stare at her, trying to place where I know her.

"Forgive me," she says, extending her hand. "I haven't introduced myself. My name is Adelpha Costas."

"Nice to meet you Mrs. Costas. I'm Maddie."

"You can just call me Adelpha."

"Alright then, Adelpha. So how did you know my mother? Were you one of her customers at the yoga studio?"

"No, no, nothing like that. Has your mother ever told you anything about her family? Where she came from?"

"Once, when I was little, I think. She said her parents died when she was young and she didn't have any siblings."

Adelpha crinkles her face. "No child, her parents are not dead. Well, one is but the other is alive and well sure as you are."

I narrow my eyes at her. "What do you mean?"

"Your mother, Calliope Costas," she pauses, wiping a tear from her cheek, "was my daughter."

I shake my head. "My mother's name wasn't Calliope Costas. It was Callie Crane."

"Callie is short for Calliope. I'm not sure why she felt compelled to change her last name, but I assure you she was my daughter and that makes you, my granddaughter."

Ok what in the actual fuck is happening? Clearly someone spiked this chic's prune juice at the old folks' home because there is no way she is my grandmother. My mom told me her parents were dead and she's never ever lied to me.

"I can see by the look on your face that you don't believe me."

"You got that right," I say, fully aware that the look on my face was probably pretty freaking close to the look Jon Snow had when Sam told him he's the one true king.

"Look, Adelpha is it? I don't know who you think you are and what you think you're doing coming to my mother's funeral with this bonkers news but I think you should leave."

She purses lips and fidgets with the pendant around her neck. She opens her mouth to say something but before she can, Erin slides into the seat next to me.

"What's going on here, Maddie?" she asks, looking at me and then at Adelpha. "Everything okay? Who's this?"

Adelpha doesn't introduce herself. Instead, she stands up, smooths her skirt and reaches for her purse, pulling out an envelope and setting it down on the chair.

"I don't want to cause you any more pain. I just felt you should know. There's a phone number and an address for me should you change your mind, if you have any questions."

She brings her fingers to her lips and then gently swipes them across my cheek before turning away and leaving. Erin waits for her to exit the hall before reaching across my lap and snatching up the envelope.

"Ok so like what the heck was that? Who was that old lady and what's with the mysterious envelope?" Erin asks.

"Um, well, she claims to be my grandmother."

"The English one? She doesn't look anything like your dad."

"No, not that one. She says she's my mom's mother. Only that's bananas because my mom told me both her parents died in a car crash when she was younger."

Erin furrows her brows and then opens the envelope, thumbing through the contents. She pulls out a slip of paper, scans it, and then sucks in a breath.

"What?" I ask.

"Yeah, what did she say her name was?"

"Adelpha Costas or something like that. She also said my mom's name was actually Calliope Costas. Why?"

Erin looks at me, like she's trying to decide she should tell me something I most definitely don't want to hear.

"Erin, what?"

"Looks like the silver haired Callie-look-alike was telling you the truth." She hands me the document. It's an original copy of a birth certificate for a Calliope Costas. I hand it back. "So? This doesn't mean anything."

"Kay, but what about these?" she says, pulling out a stack of photographs. Though they're of an adolescent girl, I'd recognize the olive-green eyes and thick matte of hair anywhere. My mother. Next, she hands me a stack of postcards addressed to Adelpha written in my mother's bubbly handwriting, and signed Callie Crane.

"Oh shit!" Erin says, covering her mouth.

"What now?" I groan.

"It looks like results from that DNA testing kit, 23 and Me. According to this, and the letter that accompanies it, you have a sister."

April 8 1991

Hey Mamma,

    I'm fine. I know you're pissed as hell and probably disappointed, but you have to know I couldn't stay. Not after what I did, especially not with the way you look at me. Anyway, I'm safe, and I'll call you when I get to wherever I'm going. Tell Daddy I love him.

    Love, Calliope

Chapter Two

I WAKE up several times in the night, which sucks because I have always been a fantastic sleeper. I once slept through an arborist trimming branches off this giant tree in the alley behind our house and one of the massive branches came crashing down into our backyard. Everyone else on the block heard it and came running out to spectate, including Mom and Rafe, but not me. Didn't hear anything. Anyway, last night I heard every creak of the floorboard, every groan of the house, and worst of all, Erin's obnoxious snoring. She gets pissed when I say she snores, but believe me, she does.

When 6:00am rolls around I say fuck it, throw off my blankets, step around Erin, who's snoring away like a buzz-saw in a sleeping bag in the middle of my floor, and yank that stupid manila envelope from Adelpha out of my messenger bag. I clamber back up to my bed, sit cross-legged in the middle and dump everything out, separating into piles. The DNA test results, my mom's birth certificate, the photographs of her as a child along with several of me growing up (wtf?) and then a heap of postcards sent from Mom to Adelpha that I arrange in chronological order. In total there are about thirty, beginning with one sent from Yreka in California dated April 21, 1991. It's signed "Calliope" which I still maintain was not my mom's name, but the handwriting on this postcard and all the others is unmistakably hers. Following the time line, she sent a postcard every few months from various towns up and down the I-5, and most of them start and end the same way- "I'm safe" and "Please don't be mad." No great detail in any of the postcards, until 2001, coincidentally the year I was born.

"Why's it so fucking bright in here?" Erin grumbles from inside her sleeping bag. It isn't bright in here. The light isn't even on. I pulled the curtain open a little, but even then, it still isn't that bright.

"Wakey wakey eggs and bakey," I say, throwing a pillow down at her. She grumbles some more before sliding out of her sleeping bag and sitting up, fumbling for her glasses. Fact about Erin, she hates wearing her glasses and never lets anyone besides me see her in them. I'm pretty sure not even Leonard has seen her in her glasses. It's not like they are huge and clunky. They actually frame her face pretty well, she just thinks they make her look silly, and I've learned no amount of my reassurance will make her change her mind on the matter.

"What time is it?" she asks.

"Almost 7: oo am," I say.

"Dude why are you even awake?"

"I couldn't sleep. Like at all. So, I decided to finally go through all this stuff from Adelpha."

Erin slides out of the sleeping bag and crawls up onto my bed, careful not to mix up the papers. She picks up a picture of my mom, age five and smiles. "It's seriously like looking at a picture of you."

I snag the picture from her and bring it up to my face. She's right, this does look like a picture of me when I was a kid. Same thick chestnut hair, same oval shaped olive-green eyes. I grimace and toss the picture back onto the bed because it's a reminder of just how much I grew to *not* look like my mom. Once I hit puberty, my hair started to frizz (like my dad's) and my complexion, which had always been on the olive side like my mom's as a kid, started looking a bit pasty(also like my dad). And then I just stopped growing once I hit 5'5, whereas my mom was a tall slender 5'9, oh and let's not even talk about the fact that she was well endowed and I didn't grow beyond a B cup. Thanks, William Crawly genetics.

I go back to skimming through the postcards. After the one dated 2001, it appears that the frequency with which she wrote decreased greatly to once a year, and all of them basically say the same variation of information-*Maddie is great, things in Ashland are good, yoga studio is still prosperous, Rafe is amazing.*

"I just don't get it, Erin. Look at all these postcards. They are clearly written by my mom, and all of these-" I hand her the latter postcards, "- are about me. Why didn't she tell me about my grandmother?"

"I think you need to talk to Rafe," Erin says.

"You think he knows about Adelpha?"

With the craziness of the funeral service and then the added confusion of meeting Adelpha, I hadn't yet been able to talk to Rafe. After the service he spent the rest of the evening in his art studio.

"Seems like he would, I mean, he was with your mom for what? Ten years? If anyone would know it would be him, don't you think?"

I shrug. "I guess. This is all just too weird."

"Understatement of the century." Erin's phone starts ringing. She rummages through her bag and winces when she finds it and answers.

"Hey Daddy, before you say anything, I know I didn't call and tell you I was staying the night with Maddie. No, I'm not at Leonard's! No, I'm not lying. Seriously?" She pulls the phone away from her ear and thrusts it at me. "He wants to talk to you."

I take the phone from her and stifle a laugh. "Good morning Mr. Whitney. Yup, she stayed with me last night. I was just so distraught. I really didn't want to be alone. No Mr. Whitney, Leonard didn't stay the night. Thank you, I appreciate it. I will tell her. Bye Mr. Whitney."

I toss the phone back at Erin. "Your dad says don't forget to go on a run today."

"OMG he is so ridic." Erin Whitney's dad really is ridic. But in a good way, I think. First of all, he's wicked hot for an older dude. That doesn't have anything to do with how ridic he is, I just feel it should be stated that Mr. Whitney is a hot older dude. He's the coach for the football team at SOU. Go Raiders. When he's not screaming the team into a victory, he's single tiger- parenting Erin and her sister Maris. In their house, academics and athletics are placed higher than anything else. You get good grades and you make varsity. Didn't matter the sport, just mattered that you were the best. Erin and Maris had both played varsity sports all four years, Maris in soccer and Erin in basketball.

The one thing he absolutely couldn't tolerate but found he really had little control over is their dating life. Maris was better at respecting the rule, but Erin, not so much. When Erin and Leonard started dating, Mr. Whitney pitched the biggest fit. Didn't matter that Leonard is super smart and the sweetest most respectable boy in the whole Rogue Valley. All boys were threats in the eyes of Mr. Whitney. One night he happened to catch Erin and Leonard hot and heavy in the back of the Subaru, so now he thinks that any time Erin doesn't come home, she's off somewhere banging Leonard.

Erin groans as she slides out of my bed and back onto the floor. "Uggg I'd better go home. Maris comes home from school tonight and Dad wants to have a family dinner."

As she rolls up the sleeping bag and gathers up her clothes, I cram everything back in the envelope and tuck it under my pillow. After Erin leaves, I pad into the kitchen for a much-needed cup of coffee and an equally much-needed conversation with Rafe. I find him bent over the sink, elbow deep inside the garbage disposal side of the sink.

"Rafe, that's meant for food, not human limbs."

He shoots me a smirk over his shoulder. "I dropped a tea bag down here and I think the string is caught on the blade. Wait, I think I got it. Huzzah!" He holds up the soggy tea bag triumphantly before tossing it in the garbage. While he washes his hands, I make a fresh pot of coffee and sit at the table to wait for him. After drying his hands, he replaces the towel on the hook and turns to leave the kitchen, but upon seeing me seated at the table staring at him, stops and turns towards me, head cocked to the side.

"Did you need something, sweet pea?" he asks.

"Yeah actually, um I wanted to talk to you about someone I met last night at the service for Mom. Do you have a second?" He looks at the clock on the wall, purses his lips, and nods.

"I have to be in the studio to meet a client, but I have a few minutes." He lowers into the seat across from me. "Tell me about this person."

"Does the name Adelpha Costas ring any bells?" He looks off to the left, as if the answer is somewhere hidden in the corner before looking back at me and shakes his head.

"Can't say that it does."

There's just enough of an influx to his voice to make me question if he's being honest. "Well, this elderly woman approached me at the service, named Adelpha Costas. She said she's my grandmother, like, she's Mom's mother. Only here's the thing. Mom always told me that both her parents died when she was young. So, there's no possible way this lady is my grandmother." I pause for a reaction. He only nods his head, so I continue. "But then she leaves an envelope with me that has Mom's birth certificate, by the way, her name was Calliope Costas, I guess. Did you know that? Oh, and she also had several pictures of Mom as a kid, a few of me as a kid, a handful of postcards written by Mom...really none of this ring any bells?"

He bites his bottom lip before responding. "No. Your mom also told me her parents were dead. It's possible she had the pictures photoshopped. People can do all sorts of crazy things when they are bored."

I shake my head. "Yeah but I just didn't get that vibe from her. As much as I hate to admit it, there was something real genuine in her expression, not to mention the fact that she's a spitting image of Mom."

"Honey I wish I knew what to tell you. I've never met anyone named Adelpha and I'm pretty sure there's no way your mom's name is really Calliope. Look, I really need to get to the studio. Can we talk more about this when I get home?"

I nod as he gets up and kisses my head in passing. I want to believe him because Rafe's never lied to me before, but there's just something off in his expression. Also, Rafe only bites his lip when he's in an uncomfortable situation, so clearly something is up. Tonight, is my monthly dinner with my dad so maybe I'll have better luck with him.

Green Leaf is packed. Mostly with college kids and their families celebrating the end of another collegiate year, but also the usual early summer tourists scoring a bite to eat before catching a play. Lucky for me, Mr. William Crawley has a standing reservation every Saturday at the same booth in the back-left corner of the restaurant, and on the first Saturday of every month, we have dinner together.

Green Leaf tends to favor the thespians, and my dad, as far as Shakespearean actors go, well, he's royalty. Up there on stage he's captivating, holds the entire audience the duration of the play, no matter the role. He just gives it his entire self, which is probably why in the parenting department, I've only ever gotten one night a month most of my life.

I elbow my way to the booth in the back of the restaurant where my father greets me with an awkward side hug. "Hi, honey it's good to see you," he says. After sliding into the booth, our usual waitress Meredith swoops in with our orders, a blackened chicken Caesar salad for Dad and a veggie burger for me.

"Thanks, Meredith," I say, sliding the plate around so I can drench the fries in ketchup. She winks at me before heading into the kitchen.

"How was the service, Maddie? I'm sorry I couldn't make it."

"It was fine. Rafe did a nice job setting it up."

He smiles and nods, hacks away at his chicken.

"You know I also graduated high school two weeks ago," I say.

"I know and I'm so proud of you."

"Would have been nice, you know, to have had you there," I say.

"I know," he says, mouth full of lettuce. "And I'm sorry. We had mandatory dress rehearsals." No rehearsal was mandatory when you were the King of Shakespeare.

"So, Maddie, tell me what your plans are for the summer. Will you be working at the ticket booth again this year?" he asks.

"No, I think I'm just going to work at Rare Earth. I'll let some of the theater interns take my schedule."

"That's a shame. I know Connie was looking forward to working with you again this summer." Connie is his on-again, off-again girlfriend who manages the festival. I shrug. "Yeah well, I'm sure she'll find an intern to cling on to. I really just want to work in the shop and hang out with Erin and Leonard before school starts in the fall."

"Remind me again, honey, what school are you going to?"

Father of the year right here, folks. Can't even remember which college his only daughter will be attending even though I sent him info about it at least thrice.

"University of Oregon, Dad."

"Ah, yes. Your friends Erin and Leonard will also be attending, is that right?" Oh sure, he can remember where *they* are going but not me. I take a long slow drink from my cola before answering.

"Erin will, Leonard will be at OSU in Corvallis."

"You know, if you want to take a gap year, you are more than welcome to accompany me on tour. You'd also be welcome with your grandmother in Surrey. She misses you so much."

Hmmm, let's think about this. A year being schlepped along from hotel to hotel, having to sit front row at a million different theatrical productions, or jet off to England (that part wouldn't be so bad) to spend a year with a stuffy grandmother I've only actually met a handful of times. Hard pass. To both.

"Thanks, Dad but I'm good with sticking around here. But there was something I wanted to talk to you about."

"What's that, dear?" he asks.

"I met a woman at Mom's memorial service. Her name is Adelpha Costas," I pause to await a reaction. Only the slight twitch of an eyebrow. "She claims that she's my grandmother. Mom's mother. Know anything about that?"

A thousand minutes pass before he responds. "I...I'm sorry dear, no. That name doesn't sound familiar. Did you talk to Rafe about it?"

"Yup. He says he's never heard of her. But Dad, she gave me a birth certificate, and photographs and postcards, and I know that she could have just as easily photoshopped everything but it doesn't seem like she did. You sure you don't know anything about her?"

"Honey, really, I don't. I loved your mother. We had an amazing time together but your mother was a very private person when it came to her life before we met, and truthfully, I think I was too self-absorbed to really pry into any details of her past. We lived in the moment and that's all we needed."

I don't know what else to say. The two people who might have known Mom even better than myself were of no help. Neither have any idea who Adelpha is, or at least claim to have no idea. At this point I can't tell if they're being honest, but there's just something not lining up. We finish the rest of our meal, making small talk, say our goodbye's and I head home to consult my good friend Google.

I had just typed her name into the search engine and am about to click Enter when there's a gentle knock on my bedroom door. Without waiting for a reply, the door opens and Rafe pops his head in.

"Hey Maddie, you have a second?" he asks.

I close my laptop and swivel in my chair. "Sure, Rafe. What's up?"

"So I need to go to Portland early tomorrow morning to meet with a gallery manager, but before I go I think we should talk about the woman at your mom's service."

"Um okay, sure."

He pushes the door open wider. "Can we talk about this downstairs?" He motions for me to follow him. What's so important he couldn't have talked to me in my room? When we get to the kitchen I stop, startled to find my dad sitting at the kitchen table nursing a bottle of Prosecco.

"Hey Dad, what are you doing here?"

"Rafe and I need to have a conversation with you. Can you sit down? It's better if you're sitting."

"No way. The last time someone told me to sit down for a conversation was when Mom told me she was dying."

"Fair enough," Rafe says, pulling up a seat to the table. After a second, I feel like an idiot being the only one standing, so I pull out a chair and slump into it with a huff.

"Okay. I'm sitting. What's going on?"

Rafe looks at my dad, who responds with a shoulder shrug. Then they just stare at each other. They are either having an epic staring contest and want me to judge, or they are both waiting for the other to start the conversation. Either way, it's super freaking annoying. Finally, my dad takes a sip from his drink, clears his throat.

"It's time for you to know the truth," he says.

Knew it. "Truth about what?" I ask.

"About the woman you met at your mother's service. Adelpha Costas." He stops and I motion for him to continue. "Honey, she *is* your grandmother. Long ago, when I first met your mother, a young carefree sprite, she provided very little detail as to her upbringing other than she grew up in California. She never talked about her family and I never asked. What I told you at the restaurant was true. I was too self-absorbed to know. However, it was when she was pregnant with you that I learned of her mother, and about their lack of relationship, and met her when she came up here for your birth."

"Why did you lie?" I ask.

"Because your mother asked me to," he replies.

"What? That doesn't make sense."

"I know," he continues. "You see, Callie and her mother were never very close. There was some rift between them and when I asked why they didn't get along, she'd deflect. Her mother came up after you were born and I don't know what happened, but one day when I came home from work Adelpha was gone. When I asked where she'd gone to, your mother said only that we would never see her again and that I was never to tell you that she existed."

"I'm sorry, but that just sounds ridiculous." I look to Rafe for some sort of clarity. "Rafe? Did you know all of this?"

"Unlike William, I pried. I wanted to know everything about your mother. Who she was as a child, where she grew up, about her family. She told me she had a mother with whom she was not on speaking terms, didn't want to say what had happened, only asked that you not be told about her. I met Adelpha only once, and it didn't go very well. I have not seen her since, but I did write to let her know about your mother's death."

"And you both went along with this? This stupid request of hers?" I ask.

"I wanted to respect your mother's wishes," Rafe says.

"And I was..." William begins but I throw up a hand to cut him off.

"Yeah yeah I know, you were too self-absorbed. This is just so crazy! So Mom has this family somewhere in California, and she never once told me about them. How could she do this? Wait, what about the DNA test results from some lady claiming to be Mom's daughter?"

Rafe and William stare at one another dumbfounded. "What are you talking about?" Rafe asks.

"Adelpha gave me DNA test results from a lady named Shasta Green claiming to be Mom's daughter."

"I knew about Adelpha," William says, "but I promise you I know nothing about her having had a child prior to our relationship."

"Honey, did Adelpha leave you any contact information?" Rafe asks. "Perhaps you should call her and talk to her."

Because that wouldn't be an odd conversation. The last and only time we saw each other I basically told her to fuck off. "I think I just need some time to digest this. It's too much."

"We understand," Rafe says, reaching across the table for my hand but I jerk it away.

"No, you don't," I say, pushing away from the table and bolting up to my room.

I don't end up doing an internet search. I just don't have it in me. Instead, I flop face down on my bed and cry myself to sleep. For eighteen years I thought my mom and I were tight. No lies, no secrets. Just honesty. We didn't even fight. Any time I'd get mad or frustrated about something Mom would bust up laughing, and then I'd naturally start laughing. Pretty soon I'd forget why I was so upset.

Now, I know that there are times when parents have to lie to their kids, like those harmless little white-lies that are told to protect someone. Excuse me if I just don't see how this situation is one of those "oh but we lied to you to protect you" kind of situations. I'm pretty sure I asked a million times if my mom had any relatives. In fact, I know I had to ask her for a school assignment. You know, one of those family tree assignments. For my dad's tree, every single branch was filled and I'm pretty sure we traced his lineage back to the King of freaking England. My mom's side however was a big fat heap of nothing. A tree with zero branches. No parents, no aunts, uncles, or cousins. And I actually believed her. Why wouldn't I though? We never think our parents are actually lying to us when we ask and they answer.

Okay whatever. Mom lied. But why make sure that both Rafe and William never told me? Is Adelpha some kind of heinous bitch? Was she hands down the world's worst mother and that's why my mom severed ties? Was she part of the Manson Family? Was she like the grandma in that old *Flowers in the Attic* movie? Something major happened between the two of them, and I have a feeling whoever this Shasta Green person is had a little something to do with it.

The next day at Rare Earth, I tell all of this to Erin and Leonard. "Mads, why don't you just call Adelpha and ask?" Leonard asks. "She left you all her contact information, right?"

I nod, folding a row of shirts. "Yeah, she wrote her address and phone number on a sticky note that was inside the envelope. I don't even know what to say, you guys. I was so cold to her at the service, and besides what if she's a not nice woman?"

"You won't know for sure if you don't reach out," Erin offers.

"Your little friends are right, sweetie," a smoky voice calls out from behind the register. Roxy Schmitt, my boss. Roxy and her husband Michael, both in their mid-60's have been running this store since Michael inherited it from his parents when he was twenty-two, under the sole condition that it remain the same: eclectic, strange, and worldly. That wasn't really an issue since Michael is the definition of the word "eclectic." They work every single day with the exception of the week of Burning Man, and they sort of took my mom in when she first moved to town.

"The only way you're going to get answers is by calling her up and asking. Sure, she may be a wackadoodle but you'll never know if you don't reach out."

"Yeah, well maybe I'm better off not knowing. I mean, the more I keep thinking about this lady, wondering who she is, the more I feel upset and angry at my mom for keeping secrets and I really don't want to feel that way ya know?"

"I hear ya doll, but you listen to me, okay?" Roxy walks around the register, pushes her way through the racks of clothes to stand in front of me. Planting her warm plump hands on my shoulders, she furrows her brows and says, "Your mother was a gem, truly the sweetest most true to herself woman I've ever had the pleasure of knowing. If she didn't ever tell you about her own mother, or any other details about her past, it was for good reason. So, if you need to be angry for a while, allow yourself that feeling, but don't let it consume you. You know in your heart the person your mother was." I smile and allow her to pull me into a hug. Her scent, sandalwood and lavender instantly calm me.

"What about the alleged half-sister?" Leonard asks. "Do you want to know anything about her?"

Did I want to know anything about her? I just spent the past two days trying to wrap my head around the fact that I have another grandmother, I almost forget about the alleged half-sister.

"I'd want to know," Erin says, yanking on the end of the licorice stick she's gnawing on. "I would. Especially if said half-sibling was balls deep in Benjamins. Holla!"

I roll my eyes. "You're deplorable, Erin. I don't know you guys. I really don't know what I want to do. Sure, it could be cool to have a sister but I also think it would just be too weird."

"Just think about it, kid," Roxy says and then kisses my forehead. "We're all here to support you."

After work I walk over to the lower duck pond in the park to think. Best case scenario, both the grandmother and the half-sister are totally chill and we instantly get along and now I have this instant family. Worst case scenario, one or both of them suck balls and then I'll feel I have to maintain a relationship out of obligation. I hate to do anything out of obligation. When I do something, either for myself or another person, I want it to be because I knowingly made that choice to do so, not because I feel guilty or because I feel I *have* to. Then there's this other part of me, when not being totally pissed at my mom, that feels I'm in some way dishonoring her memory or whatever by reaching out to Adelpha. If Mom had wanted me to know this woman, she'd have told me about her. Mom was always a good judge of character. She could read auras, as cheesy as that sounds, and could tell when a person was being genuine versus a total poser. She was also excellent at weeding out toxic people from her life. Maybe her own mother was one of those toxic people.

But I don't like mysteries. I Google the ending to every movie while I'm watching it, and I read the last chapter of every book before I even start reading the actual book. I know, it's a terrible habit, but we all have terrible habits. Now that I know my mom had these secrets, I feel compelled to know why. What happened in her past? Why'd she have a baby and give it up? Why did she have a falling out with her mother? Why did she keep it all from me? I had planned to spend my summer in Ashland working and not doing anything that required a lot of energy so that I could recoup before school, but my curiosity and inability to live a mystery told me I was about to have other plans.

I yank my phone out from my pocket and FaceTime Erin and Leonard. "Okay I've made a decision. I'm going to go to San Francisco to meet Adelpha."

"And what about the half-sister?" Leonard asks.

"Guess I'm going to meet her too. I mean, I probably should. See if she's just bullshit-ting me. But I want to meet Adelpha first. I need to know what happened between her and my mom."

"When are you leaving?" Erin asks.

"In the morning."

"Have you contacted Adelpha?" Leonard asks.

"Uh, no. Not yet. Kinda just now decided. Guess I should call and ask her though. Either way, I wanted you guys to know where I was going in case I don't come back, you know, in case she turns out to be a geriatric serial killer or something."

Erin shakes her head. "I'm going with you."

"Erin, you can't come with me. I don't even know how long I'll be gone. It might be a week; it might be the whole summer. There's no way your dad will be okay with this."

"Yeah well there's no way I'm going to let my bestfriend drive solo to San Francisco. It's just not going to happen."

Sure enough, Erin pulls up to my house in her dad's Subaru at 8:00am with two ginormous coffees from Roasters and a bag of donuts.

"Let's hit the road, bitch!"

"OMG how did you get your dad to loan you the Subaru?" I ask, laughing.

"It wasn't easy, I'll tell you that much. There was a lot of back and forth but in the end, he decided he also didn't like the idea of you being in a big city solo. So, I just have to be back before basketball camp, I have to check in every day, and I had to promise that Leonard wasn't coming."

"Well alright then. Guess we're going on a road trip."

I text Rafe to let him know where I'm going, promising to check in all the time, and then another to Roxy saying some variation of the same thing before chucking my bags into the trunk. After sliding into the passenger seat, I shut the door and almost shit myself when a drowsy Leonard shoots up from the backseat, arms flailing.

"Whattheheckwherearewe!" he yells. His hoodie is pulled up over his head, the string so tight all I see are a nose and lips sticking out.

"Holy fuck Leonard calm down. You're at my house," I say, and then shoot a look at Erin. "I thought you said you promised your dad Leonard wasn't coming?"

She shrugs her shoulders and spreads a sly smile across her face. "Get real Mads, you know I can't go more than two days without seeing Lenny. I told my dad he was interning with his uncle this summer. No biggie."

"What happens when he calls Leonard's dad? Because you know he so totally will."

"My dad's cool with covering for me," Leonard says. Like my parent's, Leonard's parents are pretty chill when it comes to their teenager. It probably helps that Leonard is super responsible, and also that he's part of MENSA, and it could *also* be that they are just as much new agers as my mom, the total opposite of the tiger parent that is Erin's dad.

By rush hour we are in the Bay area, breaking and accelerating and honking our way through the crazy busy streets, only cussing out Google Maps a few times for the wrong turns. When we finally pull up to the two-story house that looks exactly like the one from *Full House*, Adelpha is there, kneeling down by a flowerbed, a pair of green pruning shears in one hand. The smile stretched across her face is both foreign and painfully familiar. I can't get over how much she looks like my mom.

Erin kills the ignition, pulls out the key and unfastens her seat belt. When I don't move, she shifts in her seat to face me. "You okay? You know it's not too late to go back."

"No. I need to do this."

She grips my hands. "Welp, let's go meet your grandma."

June 3 1991

Hey Mamma,

I'm in Ashland. It's a town on the border of Oregon and California. It's amazing here. The Wellsprings I'm staying at truly has such healing capabilities I never knew was even possible. I know how you feel about these kinds of things, but just know I'm okay.

Calliope

Chapter Three

ADELPHA'S house is not what I expected. I don't know, I guess because she's old I envisioned there to be a million ceramic cat statues, a grandfather clock, maybe those little doilies on the table. Instead, we walk in to find it classic, elegant, and minimal. There are two cream-colored couches in the sitting room with soft earthy throws strewn across the backs, and piled with grey and pale-yellow chevron throw pillows that match the rug in the middle of the floor. On the wall behind one of the couches is an oil painting of the Golden Gate bridge separated into three sections, and a nighttime shot of the city skyline hung behind the other couch. It seriously looks like something you'd see in one of those home décor magazines. Definitely didn't look lived in.

She leads us down a narrow hall to a large brightly lit kitchen. The walls are beige, which ordinarily I wouldn't have thought would go well with white cabinetry, but there's something about it that works. The nobs on all the doors to the cabinets and pantry are the little crystal antique kinds, coincidentally the same kind we have in our house.

Nestled into the nook of a large window is a small oak table where a canary blue tea kettle and a tray of assorted teas are arranged. We clump together along the wall waiting for further instruction. Adelpha, having picked up our nonverbal ques, wipes her hands on the front of her dress, pads to the table and sets out four mugs.

"Would you all like some tea? You won't find any coffee in here, but I've got quite the selection of strong teas."

"Thank you," I say. "Tea would be nice. Earl grey if you have it."

"If you have it, she says," Adelpha chuckles, and then thumbs through her vast collection of teas until she finds a small grey packet and pulls it out victoriously. "I get this specially made down the street from the gentleman who owns the tea shop. Best with a dash of milk and just a little sugar. What about you two?" She looks up at Erin and Leonard. I have to hide a smile. Leonard loves tea just as much as I do, but Erin is a coffee drinker through and through. There's no way she's going to make it in the morning here without coffee.

"I'd love some jasmine tea, Mrs. Costas," Leonard says. She nods and then looks to Erin.

"Uh, I'll pass. I'm more of a coffee drinker."

Adelpha smirks, and pulls out a green and red packet, opening it and setting it in a mug. She pours steaming water into the mug, then hands it to Erin. "Double Irish Breakfast. Makes a fine substitute to coffee."

Erin reluctantly takes the mug. I can tell by just the swiftest glance at her face that she's preparing for a "you're wrong" moment, but thankfully she reels it in. After we've all been served, she beckons us to follow her around the corner to another room, this one looking more like a room someone lives in. A long deep chocolate leather couch hugs the wall closest to us; a similar cream-colored throw draping over one of the arms. On the other side of the living room there's a rocking chair with a plush dusty gold seat cushion. This is probably where Adelpha spends the most time, I'd say, judging on the basket full of assorted balls of yarn beside the chair, and the biggest knitting needles I've ever seen protruding from one of the balls. I wonder how does she even hold them in her nimble hands.

There's a small tv resting on a stand on the wall opposite the rocker. I can hear Erin whispering to Leonard about the size of the tv, but I'm more interested in the collection of framed photographs on the lower shelf of the stand. I can tell, even from a distance that they're my mother. I want more than anything to set my mug down, run over there to investigate every single one. Study her eyes, her hair, count the freckles on her cheeks, because right about now I'm missing her something fierce and I just want to be close to her again, even if it's by touching some old photographs of her. Instead, I sandwich myself in-between Erin and Leonard on the couch while Adelpha slides into the rocker. I try my best not to continuously stare in the direction of the photographs.

"I hope your drive wasn't too hectic," Adelpha says. "I know driving in this city can be a bit much for the non-city folk."

"It wasn't so bad," I reply, taking a sip from my tea. "Erin is pretty good at maneuvering through big cities. Her mom lives in Portland."

Adelpha smirks. "Ah yes, Portland. I've never been a big fan of Portland."

"It's alright," Erin says, shrugging her shoulders. "People suck at driving, but they're chill otherwise."

"So, you all grew up together?" Adelpha asks.

"Well, Leonard and I did," I say. "Erin moved to Ashland when we were in fifth grade. We've all been best friends since then."

"That's wonderful. It's so great when friendships can be maintained throughout young adulthood."

I nod in agreement, and wait for the next question, but I really have zero interest in making small talk. Not when there were pictures of my mother right here in front of me. My eyes keep dancing back and forth and I'm hoping Adelpha will pick up on it, maybe offer to show me the photographs, but she doesn't. Or she does notice, but enjoys watching me squirm. It's probably not the latter but still, I have no idea. She's just sitting there, rocking away in her chair and sipping her tea. When she's sucked down the last drop, which honestly seems like it took her hours to do so, she slides her mug onto an end table and then clears her throat.

"So, you must have loads of questions, about me, and your mom," she says. *Finally.*

"That *is* why we drove all the way down here," Erin says, and then yelps as I pinch her in the thigh. No one ever accused Erin of having perfect manners.

"Your friend's got spirit," Adelpha chuckles.

"That she does," I say. "So, have you lived in San Francisco your whole life?"

"Not entirely. I was born in Greece, but shortly after my birth, my family came over by boat and settled up in Mid-Market. My father worked in a Greek deli, working his way up until the owner, who had no sons or daughters of his own, passed it on to him when he died. It was then passed on to my brother, and his children run it today."

"Did you work there at all?" Leonard asks.

"Me? Oh no. I wasn't much for food service. I went to nursing school. Retired ten years ago."

"That's cool you were a nurse," I say.

"Yes, I found it to be a fulfilling life choice. It's where I met my husband, who was a doctor. He passed away several years ago, from old age, peacefully in his sleep."

Well at least it wasn't from cancer. We spend the rest of the evening flipping through various photo albums of Adelpha's family, both extended back in Greece and the ones in America. She talks on and on about her sibling and what it was like to grow up in the city, about the day she met her husband, their travels around the world while he was part of Doctors without Borders. She only briefly mentions life with my mother, and when I'd ask her to elaborate on a particular story, she'd smile and say, "We'll get to that later," only later never came. She finds different ways to get side tracked, almost like she's hell-bent on pumping me with information on her before mentioning anything about my mom.

Somewhere around seven pm she takes a break to prepare what she calls a "modest dinner" but believe me when I say there's nothing modest about it. Roasted lamb with a lavender butter drizzle, garlic asparagus, three types of bread rolls, and a few Greek dishes I have no idea how to pronounce. I don't even know how she had time to prepare it all; she was only in the kitchen for thirty minutes tops, but she assured me it took no time at all. While we eat, she asks us all about our lives, how we like living in Ashland, what are our hobbies, where Leonard and Erin's families originated from, did we like camping, what we like to eat. Still no mention of my mother. Clearly, she's playing the long game and any information I expect to get about the life of my mom will be slow coming.

At half past ten, she leads us upstairs and stops outside the first door to the left, resting a hand gently on the door. "Maddie, you and Erin can sleep in your mother's bedroom. I've put on fresh sheets. Leonard, you'll be across the hall in the guest room. The bathroom is there, at the end of the hall. I'll be downstairs."

We take the stack of fresh towels from her free arm. "Thank you, Adelpha. For dinner, and for letting us stay. I'm sure you didn't expect three visitors," I say.

"Nonsense. You're my granddaughter. You and your friends are welcome." She kisses us each gently on the forehead and pads back downstairs, using the railing for stability.

Leonard turns the knob to his room and pops his head in to inspect. "Ah. And here are where all the old lady cat figurines are." Erin and I giggle as we push past him into the room. Sure enough, three shelves secured to the wall house about ten different ceramic cats. Beneath the shelves, a small three-drawer dresser where more figurines rest on top, only these weren't cats, but instead they looked like delicate cherubs, and dancing figurines.

Aside from the ceramics, the rest of the room is sparsely decorated. Just a twin sized bed with a floral quilt, and a desk in the corner beneath the only window. I pat Leonard on the arm.

"Welp, it's a good thing you like cats. Enjoy your room. C'mon Erin, let's go see what we can learn about Callie Crane."

When I open the door, it's like I've portaled back to the '90's. I fully expected for this room to look just like the other one. I mean, it has been YEARS since my mom slept here. It only seemed logical to box everything up and make this a quilting room or something. But nope, it seems she's left it exactly the same way my mother left it. Nirvana and Pearl

Jam posters taped to the walls. Flannel shirts draped over the posters of a full-sized bed. Evidently my mother went through a sizeable grunge phase.

Erin runs her fingers across a stack of dusty cassettes on a shelf. "OMG look at all these cassettes. Mudhoney, Violent Femmes, Pixies, Sonic Youth, Pearl Jam, Hole, Stone Temple Pilots, The Smiths? Wow your mom's teenage musical taste is vastly different to the music she used to listen to as an adult."

"Right? Who knew she was into grunge and moody broody?" The adult Callie Crane rolled with the New Age and Americana musical scene. Alex De Grassi, Deep Forest, Bob Dylan, Emmylou Harris, or any drum circle ever. I didn't even think she knew who Pearl Jam was, and I'd never *ever* seen her wear anything flannel. So needless to say, I find her bedroom to be a total shocker.

Next to the bed there's a desk covered in at least twelve layers of dust, but above the desk there's a tack board littered with concert ticket stubs, articles clipped from *Rolling Stone*, and pictures of her and various friends. Her long chestnut hair always pulled to the side and braided, black converse shoes or Doc Martens, and a flannel shirt tied around her waist. A smile stretched across her face and eyes that sparkled, lined in a thick layer of black liner, totally basking in the company of her friends, which was the one thing she did carry with her into her adult life. No matter where we were or what we were doing, which usually had to do with her yoga practice, she was smiling, and surrounded by people.

I open the closet door and find it jam packed with more flannels, band t-shirts, shoe boxes stacked and stuffed with photographs and handwritten notes from friends.

As I pull down a few boxes and thumb through the contents I wonder what could have happened here, in her home life to cause her to upend herself, move to Oregon and basically recreate her entire identity?

I put the boxes back in the closet and close the door. "I don't even know what to say." I yank a photo from the cork board. "It's like she was this whole other person but at the same time she wasn't, you know? It's like her whole entire personality went through a complete metamorphosis."

Erin shrugs her shoulders. "Or maybe not. Maybe she just evolved. That's what we do ya know? As time passes, as culture and society changes, we adapt, we mold, we change. She left the grunge scene for the hippy scene. It's not unheard of, Mads."

"I know, I just feel like this person here, this teenage Calliope, is someone I don't know."

"Well that's why we're here. To get to know her."

She unzips her duffel and pulls out a small toiletry bag. "Which we will most def. do tomorrow. I'm beat as hell."

After taking turns in the bathroom, we climb into my mom's old bed. Erin drifts off to sleep within seconds, but I lay there wide awake, no matter how hard I clench my eyelids together. I feel weird and uncomfortable. I know this is where my mom slept as a child, so it should be comforting, but it's the same feeling I get in a hotel bed or an Air BnB. Sleeping where strangers have slept, and the Callie Crane who used to sleep in this bed was a stranger. I pull the comforter tightly around myself and do the only thing I feel I can do at this moment. Cry.

***

We've been with Adelpha for a week and we still haven't talked about my mother. Not in any great detail anyway. Every question asked is either dodged or answered in some cryptic way that usually leaves me with more questions. The first few days I found it frustrating because all I wanted was information on Mom, but every time Erin and I attempted to go through her bedroom closet, I'd have a mini panic attack and we'd stop. It was like there was some funky mental block keeping me from combing through all those boxes. Any information I was going to get, had to come from Adelpha, but it was clear to see she was going to continue to play the long game.

I decide to play along, and find I'm actually enjoying getting to know her. She's kind, and warm, and cooks the most amazing meals from scratch. When she laughs, it comes from deep down in her belly, and Leonard has taken to her because she loves science just as much as he does.

Erin on the other hand, well, she's hating this trip because it's a known fact that Erin has zero patience with just about anything. She wants answers, sometimes it seems almost more than I do, and it's taking every fiber of my being to keep her from lashing out at an old woman.

"Maddie, I just don't get it. Like, what's her angle? She wanted you to come down here and get to know her, get to know your mom but so far all she's done is schlepped us around to farmers markets and the Warf. I don't even like fish!"

Adelpha wanted to make sure we saw every square inch of the city so we hopped from train car to train car hitting up all the farmers markets she loves, and to her old neighborhood, introducing us to all of her extended relatives, of which there are many.

"I know Erin, I don't know what to tell you but I kinda feel like this is more of a catch a fly with honey situation. Maybe if we continue to spend time with her, getting to know her, she'll feel ready to talk about my mom."

"Mads, it's been a full week and we've gotten nowhere. It just feels like she's never going to tell you anything useful, and before you know it, it's time to head back home for college."

"Babe, this trip is also about getting to know who her grandmother is, ya know?" Leonard's offer is met by a glare. Erin hates to be corrected.

"I get that, and that's cool but I just don't know how much more I can take."

"Well you don't have to be here. I'm more than capable of doing this on my own." I hadn't meant for it to come out as clipped as it had, but it's enough to piss her off. She waves her hands at me, puffs up her cheeks and storms off the porch.

"I'll go talk to her," Leonard says, and then takes off down the steps after her. They return an hour later while Adelpha and I are in the kitchen preparing dinner.

"Mads, can we talk to you?" Erin asks, fingers interlocked with Leonard's. I wipe my hands on a kitchen towel and follow them out to the front porch.

"What's up?" I ask, glancing back and forth between the two of them. They share a look and then Erin sucks on her lower lip before spitting it.

"Okay so first off, I'm sorry for storming off. That was totally lame of me."

"It's okay. I get it."

"Second," she continues, "Lenny and I have been talking and we think if you're cool with it, you know, comfortable enough with Adelpha, we're gonna spend a few nights on our own and check out the city. Give you and your grandma some space to continue getting to know each other."

I'm not sure if I should feel pissed at being ditched or grateful for the space. I know it's Leonard's idea, because there's no way Erin would ever think of leaving me here with a woman I barely know, but at the same time, I could see in her face how much she wanted it. We were sisters, but we both knew we needed space. Also, who wouldn't love the idea of spending a few nights in a big city with your boyfriend? Not that I've ever had a boyfriend, in the real sense of the term, I guess. I dated a guy named Kyle Wolf who was the student council president for Junior year, but it was kind of off and on, only in groups, and we only made out twice. Yup, I "dated" him a whole year and we made out twice. That's it. Pretty pathetic if you ask me, so yeah, if I *did* have a real boyfriend, I'd want to have an epic big city date night.

"I mean, if you guys are sure, I'm okay with it," I say. "I'll be fine here with Adelpha."

"Okay, so we'll be back in two days. You *sure* that's fine?" Leonard asks, placing a hand on my shoulder and squeezing. Leonard is only six months older than me, but he's always treated me like a little kid. Probably because he has like seven little sisters. Sometimes it's annoying but mostly it's nice.

"You'll be fine with us going off to explore the city without you?" Erin asks.

"I'm more than okay with it," I say, bringing them in for a group hug. They wait until after dinner before packing an overnight bag and heading out. Adelpha insisted they take snacks, and by that she really meant containers full of left overs. Once they've left, Adelpha and I settle into the living room to work on a puzzle. She brings out a tray of tea and cookies and hands me one of the mugs.

"I'm sorry your friends left. I do hope it wasn't because of something I said."

"Oh no it didn't have anything to do with you," I fib. "She and Leonard hardly ever get alone time together. Her dad is pretty strict, so she just wanted to get away with him for a day or two."

"It doesn't bother you? To be ditched?"

"Nope. I'm not really the jealous possessive friend type."

She sips from her tea, nodding, and probably not believing a word I say. Sure, sometimes when the three of us are hanging out, there *might* be times when I feel third-wheel-ish, but I'd never let it develop into anything more. Certainly not anything resembling jealousy.

"Really. It's never been a big deal. We're all good at making time for one another and just making sure no one is left out. Plus, Erin's dad has always kept her so busy with school and sports. She isn't even allowed to go on dates with him unless it's a group date."

"Ah he's one of those parents. Tell me about him."

I swallow the bite of cookie that was in my mouth, take a scalding drink of my tea, and wait for my throat to stop burning.

"Mr. Whitney. Single dad to two amazingly beautiful daughters, head football coach at Southern Oregon University, super into organization and prioritizing, especially when it comes to his daughters' lives, um, very overprotective, and generally not trusting of the male sex, at least not when it comes to his daughters."

Adelpha chuckles. "And where's the mother? Is she not around?"

"She is sort of. Remember I said she lives in Portland? Erin really only sees her on holidays and some three-day weekends. They split up when Erin was nine. Her mom stayed in Portland and the girls moved with Mr. Whitney to Ashland when he got the job at the university."

"And she's a good friend to you?"

"Absolutely. She's like a sister to me. We fight and all that like normal friends do, but we have each other's backs."

She nods and sips from her tea. "Tell me more about Rafe."

I thumb a puzzle piece, thinking about what to say in the way of an answer. Rafe said they'd met only once and that it didn't go well. I don't want to say anything that might set her off, and I also don't want to hear her say anything disparaging about him.

"Well, what do you want to know?" I ask, connecting the puzzle piece.

"He's not your father but you seem to regard him as such, so I'd like to hear about him. How he became such an important figure in your life and in your mother's life."

"Uh okay. Well, Mom met him when I was about five, I think, when he leased the open space next to her yoga studio and turned it into an art studio. They were friendly neighbors at first and then started dating. I think like a year later he moved in and he's been with us ever since."

"What does your father think of him? You still speak to your father, yes?"

"Oh yeah. Once a month during Shakespeare season we have dinner together. He likes Rafe. He doesn't think he's been replaced or whatever, and if he did, I wouldn't know because he's not really around to say so."

"How does that make you feel?"

OMG were we in a therapy session? "I feel fine about it. He is who he is and I have always had Rafe for all the dad stuff, so it's never been a big deal." She twitches an eyebrow up and leans forward in her chair to place a puzzle piece.

"You've never felt abandoned by him or angry that he decided his career as an actor was more important than raising his child?" she asks.

"Yeah, sure, maybe a little. But that's his problem. I don't have "daddy issues" or anything if that's what you're trying to get at."

She takes a long sip from her tea. "I knew your father. Back before you were born." She pauses, and when I don't say anything, continues.

"Your mother was such a charismatic young woman. Always looking for the next big thing, always seeking adventure, and that included with the young men she spent her time with. I remember when she met William Crawley. She sent me a post card from one of the first productions he was staring in. Hamlet, if I'm not mistaken. She said she stumbled into the most handsome man at the farmer's market and it was love at first sight."

I do a mental scan of all the postcards I'd read from the stack in the envelope, trying to picture the one she's talking about, but nothing comes to mind. "I don't remember reading that one."

"That's because I didn't include it." She hoists herself from the chair and pulls down a floral box from the top of the bookshelf next to the television. After swiping off the dust, she removes the lid, shuffles through the contents and procures a postcard, sliding it across the table in front of me. Gingerly I pick it up and examine the picture on the front. It takes me a moment to see it, but there he is. A younger version of my dad hidden behind layers of tulle and plushy vibrant fabric, holding up a grey skull in his left hand.

"Why didn't you include this one?" I ask.

"Well, in the event you chose not to believe me and then burned the contents of the envelope, I saved some for myself."

"Here's what I don't get. If my mom disliked you so much that she didn't even tell me about you, why'd she go through the effort of sending you all these postcards?"

"Our relationship had always maintained a hefty layer of tension and frustrations, even from the day she was born. She came out fists clenched and an angry scrunched up face that didn't relax for weeks. I think the post cards were her way of maintaining communication the best way she knew how."

"My father said he'd met you, so you must have at some point reunited, you and mom."

"When your mother called me to say she'd given birth to you, she was a right combination of terrified and excited, which his normal for all new mothers. I was nervous for her, because the last time she had a child, she felt she didn't have what it takes to be a mother-" she pauses and puts up a hand, having seen my mouth open and ready to blurt out a question. "I'll get to that in a moment," she continues. "When she told me you'd been born, and that she intended to keep you, I bought a bus ticket to Ashland to see her, help her where I could be of service. Your father picked me up at the bus station and right away I could see why your mother had been so taken by him. Smart, devilishly handsome, a real charmer. Your mother, she was so smitten with you, the way she kept you tucked up into her chest, how she cooed at you, I knew without a doubt that she was meant to be your mother. But when your father held you, though his eyes twinkled and his smile was bright, there was something about the way he held you, kind of at a distance, like he wasn't quite sure what to do with you. I knew early on that he wasn't ready to be a parent."

"Did you tell my mom?"

"Not then. We were already on such shaky ground. I did tell her some days later."

"What happened then? When you told her?" I ask.

"She said I didn't know what I was talking about and after a spat, felt it best I go. Your father drove me to the bus station and that was it. No more calls, no more postcards for some time. When your father left for good, you were three. She had called, first time in two years, to say she was scared to be a single parent. So, I returned to help her. We were fine at first, found a rhythm, the three of us. One day your father returned to gather some things and tend to some affairs with a production."

"For a time, your mother forgot he was going to leave again, and when he did, she was devastated. I reminded her of what I'd told her years ago- that from day one I knew he wasn't meant to be a father and that while he was a charmer, he was nothing more than that. I told her she wasn't going to be able to raise a child on her own, that she was too immature and begged her to return to California. She got angry with me, said I was no longer welcome in her life and the next day I was on the bus back home to California."

"And that was the last time you guys talked?" I ask.

"No, not quite. I received one post card every year." She pulls out a postcard from the box and and hands it to me. "This one was to to say she'd met a man whom she loved, who loved you as his own, and that she was going to be okay. That was her thing. Always telling me she was going to be okay. I never believed her of course, but this time, it turned out, she really was."

"Rafe said he'd met you once?" I asked, wiping a rogue tear from my cheek.

"Yes, once. Your mother invited me to come up and meet Rafe. She said he'd encouraged her to make amends and so I agreed to come up for Thanksgiving holiday. I unfortunately did not show my best side, I said some unsavory words to Rafe. Your mother told me never to contact her again. It broke my heart."

"What did you say to him?"

"Oh, I hardly recall the exact words," she says.

I shake my head. "I just don't understand. It really just seemed like a fight that could have been worked through. She stopped talking to you because of an opinion you had, which turned out to be correct I might add, about my father?"

"I told you already that our relationship was always very complicated. She'd gotten along with her father, but never with me. There were times we'd go whole weeks without speaking when she was a teenager."

"What happened before she left for Oregon? Does it have to do with the woman who did the DNA test? Shasta Green?"

Adelpha sucks in her lips and stares off into a far corner of the room, clutching the memory box so tight I'm sure it's going to crush. After a few moments, she shifts her eyes to mine, replaces the lid on the box and rises up out of her chair.

"I think that's enough for today. I'm feeling a bit tired. I think I'll go to bed now."

Are you kidding me? We were finally getting somewhere with my mom! "Wait, Adelpha, it's only 8:00pm."

"Well I'm old, *Paidi mou*. When you're a fossil like me you'll understand why I want to retire so early." She brushes my cheek with the tips of her fingers before heading up the stairs, leaving me with a head so full of questions I feel about ready to burst.

I whip out my phone and try calling Erin but it goes straight to voicemail. I leave a message for her to call me asap and slide further into the recesses of my chair. My whole approach to getting answers is not working as well as I thought it would. I told Erin it was going to take time, that she was being too impatient, but this is getting frustrating as hell. The second she opened that box and pulled out those postcards I wanted to know everything right away. More than anything, I want her to just be straight with me, give me straightforward answers, and not drag this out anymore because she's old and tired and needs a nap.

***

I'm up before the sun the next morning. I'm pretty sure I'm even up before Adelpha. I don't hear her rattling around downstairs in the kitchen. I couldn't sleep at all last night. I kept thinking about what Adelpha had said about her encounters with my dad and Rafe, and her being in Ashland after I was born. I don't know what they argued about, and I can only imagine whatever it was she'd said to Rafe on the last day my mom saw her was something super atrocious. Rafe is such a chill, easy-going person. Everyone in town loves him, almost as much as they loved my mom. I find it hard to believe he would have provoked Adelpha. It's just not in his nature. Maybe Adelpha said something to Mom and Rafe defended her? It's the only way he would have said anything or done anything that would result in an epic vocabulary throw-down.

Adelpha made it sound like any miniscule thing she and Mom fought over, any un-shared opinion turned into full blown battles between the two, and I know her leaving has to do with the baby she gave up. But that begs the question-why did she give her baby up? Was she not ready to be a mom? Was the baby a product of rape? I'd hate to think that's the case but Mom *did* grow up in a large city and the layout of her room tells me she had a huge wild streak.

It's too much for my brain and I know Adelpha's tea isn't going to cut it this morning. There's a café up the street next to the bookstore. I am in desperate need of a strong cup of coffee.

I throw on some clothes, creep downstairs and as I'm snagging my purse from the hook by the door, Adelpha's bedroom door creaks open. She steps out, wrapping her robe around her petite frame and looks startled to see me.

"Maddie, it's not yet six. Where are you sneaking off to?" she asks.

"I'm sorry if I woke you. I couldn't sleep and I really just need some coffee. I was just gonna run down the street real quick."

She nods and offers a gentle smile. "Alright, dear. I'll make some breakfast for you for when you get back. Their food is not the best."

I know by now she'd say that about any food that wasn't whipped up by her. "Thank you, Adelpha but if it's alright with you I'd rather just grab a scone or something to go with my coffee." She frowns, and I hope I haven't hurt her feelings.

"How about you wrap something up for me and I'll heat it up when I get back? You know, in case I don't like the scone?" I say.

Her frown turns into a soft smile. "That can be arranged. Mark my words, you will not like their scones."

I smile at her, and head out. It's a five-minute walk, but I stretch it to ten. I'm not in any rush. The second I walk in I'm enveloped by the aroma of freshly roasted coffee beans. How I've lived off of strong black tea these past several days is a mystery. I order the largest mocha they have, a blueberry scone and find a small table tucked into the back of the shop. While I wait for my coffee to cool a bit, I take a bite from the scone and immediately spit it into my napkin. Adelpha was right. This scone is horrible.

I push the abomination they call a scone off to the side and pull out my phone to catch up on obligatory texts. I send one to Rafe to check in, being completely vague about everything, and one to Michael and Roxy to make sure things were going okay at Rare Earth. I send a text to Erin, letting her know Adelpha finally cracked and to call me when she wakes up. I've just started to scroll through Ashland news when she calls.

"Are you freaking kidding me?" she says, mouth full of something. "I leave and then she starts giving you the facts? Wow. Just...wow."

"I know. And then I asked her about you know, the baby Mom gave up and the old lady clammed up. Said it was time for bed. It was 8pm!"

"Ugg what is it with old people and early bed time?"

"I know right? Anyway, I couldn't sleep and really just wanted a good cup of coffee, so I left before six. I'm down at that coffee shop by her house. You'd like it. I might check out the bookstore next door before I head back. Hello! Erin? Are you paying attention?" She'd been making muffled giggling sounds in between her "mhmms" and "Uhhuhs".

"Oh yeah sorry, Mads. It's Leonard...anyway I'm sorry she's been so lame about this."

Before I can respond, she lets out a playful squeal and then it sounds like an echo through water. She's more than likely dropped her phone. Cool and all that she and Len are having a great time, but for one second I'd like a little of her attention. Frustrated, I hang up, shove the phone into my messenger bag, and head out. The bookstore hasn't opened yet, so I go back to Adelpha's. I knock twice and then open the door, stopping at the sound of laughter coming from the kitchen. "Hello? Adelpha?" I call out.

"In the kitchen Maddie," she replies. I set my bags down on the bench by the door and pad down the hall to the kitchen. Adelpha is seated at the table across from someone with long chestnut hair. When the head of hair turns, I gasp. It's my mother, only not my mother. Same hair, same tan skin, same high cheekbones, and almond-shaped eyes, only hers are slightly more blue than green. Then she smiles, and holy hell it's my mom's smile. I reach out for anything to steady my balance, hand falling against the refrigerator. I know without having to be told, this is her, my mother's first-born. My ...sister. She stands abruptly, knocking the chair with her hips, grabbing it before it has a chance to fall. With her left hand extended, she walks toward me. "You must be Maddie. Hello. I'm Shasta. Shasta Green. Your, um, sister."

January 1 1992

Hey Ma,

    Still in Ashland. Sorry it's been awhile. Figuring things out. I just wanted to let you know I'm going to India with some amazing people to study yoga. Align my chakra. Get centered. Don't worry. I'll be okay.

    Namaste, Callie Crane

    p.s you're probably pissed I changed my name.

Chapter Four

WHEN I was a kid, probably starting somewhere around age seven, my mom would pack up a couple night's worth of stuff-tent, sleeping bags, yoga mats, heaping portions of granola, and load up her Subaru (basically everyone in Ashland owns Subaru's. It' a thing, I guess) and we'd take a sporadic road trip to Bend. It wasn't uncommon for Mom to wake up and decide we were heading out of town. She said it was something she'd grown accustomed to in her early 20's and felt it was truly the only way to maximize the most out of life. Be sporadic. Shake things up. Do yoga in the desert. She loved the desert, and anything near a river, so more often than not our "sporadic road trips" were somewhere in Central Oregon. She had her favorite camping spots always in full rotation, Sparks Lake, Wyeth, anywhere on the Crooked River. I've never been much for camping, but I went along, mostly because I wasn't about to let her go out into the wilderness on her own (though she'd be more than fine!) and because, I don't know, there was just something so calming and comforting about being alone with her, far from home, with just a low burning fire, wide open sky full of stars, and the sound of nature whirling all around us.

By the end of the weekend, we were stinky, disheveled, ready for modern luxuries like showers and deep-cushioned beds, but I loved how tousled she looked when we'd get home. Not only outward, but inward I could tell that she felt refreshed. Her eyes sparkled a little brighter, her skin glowed, and her aura, as silly as it sounds, seemed to radiate.

That's exactly how Shasta looks, standing there next to Adelpha. I don't mean she's stinky or anything, or that her hair is unkept, but the skin glow, the peaceful aura, it was all there. The freaking spitting image of my mother, just like Adelpha. Her smile, curling slightly to the left, wavers and I notice she's gripping her clasped hands together so tight her knuckles are turning white. She's understandably nervous. I mean, who wouldn't be nervous to meet a sister they didn't know existed?

I notice how tall she is. Mom was 5'9, but Shasta looks to be about 5'10, maybe 5'11. Her jeans are torn just above the knee and her David Bowie t-shirt hangs off her without looking like she's wearing a curtain. She's also doctored it up a bit, having cut out the collar and threaded some sort of lavender colored ribbon through holes she cut at the hem. The way she's paired it with her converse shoes, leather strap bracelets, and nose ring, she looks so much like the teenage Callie from the pictures in her bedroom. Here I am, a measly 5'5 wearing cargo shorts and plain white t-shirt. She is clearly awesome and I am totally jealous. I don't even have my ears pierced because I'm afraid of how much it might hurt.

I still haven't responded to her introduction. I'm staring like a moron with my jaw slack. Internally, I'm deciding between one of two responses. I could wrap my arms across my chest, jut out a hip and stare her down before asking her who she thinks she is, claiming my mom is her mom, before ever listening to her story about how she searched high and low for her birth parent's yadda yadda yadda. It's what I really want to do. If I'm being honest. But, another part of me is thinking about Mom and what she'd do if she were alive. She'd tell me I need to forget about a handshake, go for a hug because Shasta was a human being and we treat other human beings with love and respect. Also, I'd come down here to meet both a grandmother and a sister so, no matter how much she looked like my mom (and how little it turns out I did) I needed to not act like a petulant eighteen-year-old.

I force a smile across my face, cross the threshold, arm extended, hand ready for a shake. After a visible wave of relief washes across her face (she probably expected me to go with thought-option number one), she reaches out to me, our hands sliding together. I thought her hand would be clammy, since she'd held it so tight, but it wasn't in the slightest. It was warm and soft.

"Hi. I'm Maddie Crane. Nice to meet you, Shasta." I must have been overcome by something, because before I know it, I'm pulling her into a hug, which is so totally out of character for me, but if we were going to do this, we were going to DO this. She wraps her arms around me. She smells like grapes, which is such an interesting thing to smell like. I don't even think Bath and Body Works has a lotion that smells like grapes, so it's hard to explain it in terms of lotions, but that's what I smell when I breathe her in. Sour green grapes and campfire.

"You smell like grapes," I blurt out once we've stopped hugging. She looks at Adelpha and laughs. "That's not a weird thing to say, is it? That you smell like grapes? I don't know if anyone in the history of anything has been told they smell like grapes. Guess it's better than being told you smell like a foot." I'm rambling. I need to stop rambling before she thinks her newly found sister is a total moron.

"It's not a super weird thing to say," she responds. "Well, it might be, but not for me. I own a vineyard. I grow grapes for wine so I'm basically up to my elbows in grapes." When she speaks, she gesticulates with her hands. This is not a shared quality with our mother.

"That's pretty cool. We have some great vineyards where I live in Oregon, but I'm sure they probably pale in comparison to all to the ones where you live. Napa Valley, right?"

"Yeah, that's right. I live in Calistoga. It's a pretty neat town, though they are sticklers about fast food restaurants. They aren't allowed. Can't tell you what it's like to live in a town without a Taco Bell."

Adelpha clears her throat. "Maddie, I hope you don't mind but I've invited Shasta to spend the night with us. I thought now would be a good time for the two of you to meet and get to know one another."

I wish she'd consulted with me first, but it's too late now. She's already here and what kind of person would I be to say no? "Sounds great, Adelpha," I say.

"Wonderful. Maybe you can get her situated in the room Leonard is using while I finish with the dishes."

"Oh Adelpha, if there's someone else already using the room…"

"It's okay," I interrupt. "He's not going to be back for a few days."

"If you're sure. One question though, who's Leonard?" she asks.

"My best friend. Well, one of my best friends."

"He's a charming young man," Adelpha says, filling the sink with warm water. "Just don't get into a conversation about anything science related."

"Got it," she says, smiling.

"He's spending a few days with his girlfriend, my other best friend Erin, in the city. They wanted to give me some time with Adelpha."

"That makes sense. I'll go get my bags from the car. Be right back."

Once she returns, she follows me up the stairs and I show her to the guest room. Thankful Leonard is a neat freak and left it the way he'd found it. She dumps her bag on the bed, and we head downstairs to the living room where Adelpha has left a tray of muffins and iced tea.

"I love this house," Shasta says, plopping down on the couch next to the city scape paintings. "It's laid out so neat and everything seems to have a story."

"Yeah it's cool."

This is the part where we are supposed to make small talk, typically required when meeting a new person, but I hate small talk. I suck at it. I'm much better with the deep, soul-searching conversations, and I know in order to get to that place with a person you have to first meet them and get past the awkward small talk, but I suck at it. Dad says it's the Brit in me, whatever that means. He lives for small talk though, so his statement is garbage.

"This is awkward," she says, as if reading my mind.

I shift, crossing my left leg over my right, and then switching them. "Yeah, a little bit," I say, and she raises an eyebrow at me, pulling her lip up into a grin. "Okay, a lot. It's a lot...awkward."

"Well, why don't we just start with the basics. I'll tell you about me, my life in Calistoga, you can tell me about you and your life in Ashland, and when we're ready, we'll talk about...our mother. Sound like a plan?"

There's something about the flow of her voice, the way it starts out kind of low and raspy before fluctuating to a high sing-song tone that I find interesting. Not comforting, like the way most people would agree Morgan Freeman's voice is, but interesting, like I want to listen to her tell me about the history of vineyards, which I mean, she could because she grows grapes for a living.

"I'll go first," she says, taking a drink from her iced tea. "Okay so I already told you I grow grapes on a vineyard. We don't make the wine or anything, which is probably confusing since we're called Sweet Briar Cellars. It's been in my husband's family for as long as anyone can remember. At one point in time, they made wine, but now we just grow the grapes and sell them to local wineries." She takes another drink before continuing.

"I'm 28, I have a husband named Steven, he's also 28 and he manages the business end of the vineyards while I manage the growing and harvesting of the grapes."

"That's pretty cool," I say. "I like that the roles are kinda flip-flopped. You out in the fields, your husband in the office. That probably sounds sexist or whatever."

"Nope, not at all. I've always been fascinated with horticulture. My parents used to own an olive farm in Ojai so it's just been second nature to me. It's actually what I went to school for at UC Davis, which is where I met Steven. We both majored in plant science."

"Plant Science? I didn't even know that was a major."

"Oh yeah. It's pretty big here in Cali. Lot of great schools for it."

"What made you choose UC Davis?" I ask.

"My dad is an alumnus, guess that was the biggest influence. What about you? You just graduated high school, right? Any plans for college in the Fall?"

"Well, I got into University of Oregon, and I'm supposed to be going there in the Fall, but..."

"But you aren't ready to go?" she asks.

"Something like that. Lately I've been thinking about taking a gap year. They said I could do a default admission or whatever. I just...I think I need a break before diving into four plus years of higher education." She doesn't ask why, but I think she's figured it out.

"Do you know what you want to study when you do decide to go?" she asks instead.

"Not really. I mean, I feel like I should major in something practical, something that I know I'll be able to find a job in once I graduate, like psychology or criminology but I feel a pull towards creative writing. I don't know what in the way of a stable career that leads to, but it's just what calls to me."

"Well, I am a firm believer in following one's passion, even if it doesn't end up working out. Believe it or not but before I went to UC Davis for horticulture, I went to design school because I've always loved fashion and making my own clothes. I watched like every episode of *Project Runway* and was convinced that's what I wanted to do, be a professional designer."

"I'm guessing it didn't go very well if you ended up on a vineyard?" I asked.

"Oh yeah I bombed. Big time. Turned out design was more a hobby and not a profession for me."

For the next hour we sit in Adelpha's living room swapping stories, getting to know one another. I tell her about Rafe and his art studio, my theatrical sometimes-father William Crawley, the grandparents in England I hardly know, and about growing up in Ashland. She tells me more about her husband Steven, about their lives in Calistoga, and about their five- year- old daughter Sarah. Her face beams as she talks about her, the tangled mess of red ringlets, the dusting of freckles across her nose that look like the Big Dipper, and her fascination with cars and trucks. Then she talks about her childhood. She has a great relationship with her adoptive parents, Bev and Jerry Callahan, who spilled the beans about the fact that Shasta was adopted when she was ten, and about her younger sister who was a "miracle baby" since Bev had always had fertility issues.

"They tried for years to conceive but nothing worked. When they adopted me, they thought that was it for them, but six years later my mom got pregnant naturally with my sister."

"You have a sister?" I ask.

"Yup. Her name is Caroline. She's 22."

"Were you super pissed to find out you were adopted?" I ask.

"You know, I really wasn't. I mean, I had loads of questions, who were my birth parents, why didn't they want me, yadda yadda, but I wasn't upset. It explained why I look nothing like my younger sibling. I mean, she's got my dad's same silky strawberry blonde hair, ice blue eyes, and pale skin, and I don't. But Bev and Jerry were so good at loving me that eventually the fact that I was adopted didn't even seem to be something worth thinking about anymore."

"So then what made you want to seek out your birth family?"

"Last year I was sick with COVID so I spent a week in bed binge watching shows on Hulu. There was this one show about a girl who wanted to find her birth parents so she did a DNA test and found out her biological father was this sketchy doctor dude who like scammed a bunch of women at a fertility clinic."

"Scammed them how?" I interject.

"He swapped his semen for the men coming in and impregnated the women."

"Okay ew, Go on," I say.

"Anyway, this gal finds that she has like over one hundred half siblings from this guy and I kept thinking what if I have one hundred half siblings? My mom swore up and down that my situation wasn't like theirs, they'd gone through a legit adoption agency, but I couldn't shut down my insane curiosity. So I did that DNA test thing. Thankfully it came up with one sibling match."

"So you didn't take the test just to find your birth mother?" I ask.

"I mean, not originally. I just wanted to make sure my story wasn't the same as the poor individuals on that documentary."

"So why reach out?"

She shrugs. "Curiosity? I mean, I had a great childhood with wonderful parents and a sibling to play with, but I have a daughter, and at some point she'll ask me about it, and I won't know what to say. I guess I wanted to know why my birth mother gave me up. So, if you're thinking I want something monetary out of this, either from you, or from Adelpha, I don't."

I'm not going to deny that's where my thoughts had originally gone. She found out she was adopted and she wanted to do some DNA test to try and see if her birth family came from money, and when she found out her birth mother had died, she wanted to see what she'd be entitled to. Anyone would have thought that right off the bat. You can never be too trusting in these types of situations, so yes. Admittedly I thought she wanted something out of us. Am I about to tell her that's what I think? No. Not a chance.

"I don't think that at all," I say.

She responds with a smirk. "Yes, you did. Be honest."

Well crap. "Ok fine, you caught me. I did think that, at first, a little."

"When Adelpha told me our mom died, the first thing that came to my mind wasn't oh I wonder what kind of fortune she left behind, it was more like, crap I'll never get the chance to meet her. Then Adelpha said Calliope had another daughter, I thought it might be cool to meet her, meet you."

Now she's crying and it's uncomfortable because I just can't do the whole crying thing. So instead, I suggest we go up to my mom's old bedroom so she can look through her stuff. I tell Adelpha we'll be upstairs and then I lead Shasta to the bedroom.

"Adelpha never offered to let you go through this stuff before?" I ask, opening the door and swiftly shoving my dirty laundry under the bed before Shasta enters. She scans the room, taking note of the ceiling to floor posters of The Smiths, the corkboard with concert stubs, the vanity with photographs.

"No, I mean, I've only been here a few times since I met Adelpha, back in early April, and she never showed me Calliope's room, and it never occurred to me to ask."

"Callie."

"Huh?"

"My mom's name was Callie."

Shasta tilts her head and confusion spreads across her face.

"She may have been born Calliope Costas, but Mom went by Callie. Callie Crane."

Shasta nods. "Ok. Callie it is."

I slide open the doors to the closet and pull down several boxes from the top shelf.

"So my friend and I looked through a few of these, it's mostly school stuff, notes from her friends. It got a little hard so we stopped."

"Are you sure you want to do it now?" she asks.

I sigh. "Yeah I mean, you more than anyone should know who the great mysterious Callie Crane was before she was, you know, Callie Crane."

We sift through the contents of boxes stacked in the back of the closet, the ones I couldn't bring myself to go through with Erin. I'd managed to look through the trinkets on her desk and vanity, but the farther I ventured into the closet, the more I'd start to cry. But with Shasta here, as we thumb through the boxes and sift through her closet wardrobe, I don't feel like I'm going to bawl.

Here's what else I discover whilst going through everything in detail with Shasta: my mom was a freaking hoarder. Back home, mom had been more of a minimalist. Along with fistfuls of concert ticket stubs, there are notes from her friends, probably passed to one another in the halls between classes, trinkets from various amusement parks, bus passes, trolley passes, wrist bracelets from concerts, and movie theater stubs. There are three shoeboxes alone stuffed to the brim with photographs- group pictures from school where my mom was (gasp) a smoker. It's hard to believe this was the same woman who used to stick photographs of smoke damaged lungs in my lunch boxes every day as a way to scare me from being a smoker.

Shasta leans over me and snags the picture in my hand, uttering a gasp. "Oh my God, is that Callie with Dave Gahan from Depeche Mode?"

I shrug my shoulders. While I know I can pick out Morrisey from a lineup, Depeche Mode, and the founding members (any member really) I'm less familiar with.

"I love Depeche Mode," she swoons, cradling the picture before handing it back to me. I toss it back into the box with the others and replace the lid.

"There are so many boxes of pictures. I've never seen Mom photographed so much."

"Didn't you guys have family pictures done? Or take any pictures to capture happy moments?" Shasta asks.

"Some, but not a lot. Mom really wasn't the sentimental type. I mean, she collected things, really rare pieces of art, mismatched pillows, but lining our walls with photographs really wasn't her thing."

Shasta stands and pulls down some of the clothes on hangers. "I absolutely love her style. So vintage. I guess they weren't really vintage when she was wearing them, but still."

The clothes in her closet were all dark, various shades of blacks, and greys, deep purples. And lace. Lots and lots of lace, which was a total contrast to the array of earthy colors she wore in her yoga pants and scarves. Also, no lace. Or tule. I was beginning to see that for as well as I thought I knew my mother, I really didn't know her at all.

Dinner is fabulous of course. In a million years I don't think I'd ever be able to learn how to cook like Adelpha. Mom wasn't much the chef at home. Usually, we ordered in or Rafe did the cooking. Mom could make coffee but Rafe could whip up a mean Spanish omelet in seconds. I'm wondering though, how much of mom's inability to cook without burning was an act. With the amount of lavish food Adelpha makes, how was it ever possible for my mother to grow up here and not pick something up?

I don't even know what it is that Adelpha's made, but there's a meat, she claims it's lamb, and mountains of steamed vegetables and breads with garlic butter, and mounds of roasted artichokes slathered in a lavender-butter sauce. It's so good we devour the entire meal in silence, Adelpha glancing up at us once in a while with a pleasant grin stretched across her face. Behind her smile though, I sense she's longing for that one thing she wants but would never ever get again. Her daughter.

"Did you two have a good time getting to know each other? It looks like you were finally able to go through some of your mother's belongings," Adelpha says after scraping up the last bite on her plate and wiping her mouth with her clothe napkin.

"Yes, absolutely," Shasta replies. "Maddie, I'm just so glad that you agreed to come down and meet us. I was really nervous that you wouldn't want to come. When Adelpha told me you were here, I almost didn't believe her."

"Yeah well it was a lot to process. I mean, finding out I had a long-lost grandmother and half-sister all within the same week of losing my mother was kind of heavy."

"Oh no for sure, I totally get it. I appreciate having had the opportunity to go through her stuff with you. It gave me insight to who she was, but it would have been nice to meet her."

I shake my head. The pictures upstairs, the dark clothes in the closet, that wasn't my mom. My mom was bright, and cheery, and selfless. Something happened to her here to cause her to uproot her life and basically create a whole new identity. I don't want to put Adelpha on the spot, not after she's made such a wonderful dinner, but Shasta's here and she needs to know just as much as I do about my mom.

I chug what's left of my water. "Adelpha. This has been great, this meal, getting to know you, meeting Shasta, but...I think it's time you tell me about my mom-our mom-why she left, and why she gave Shasta up for adoption." I shoot a glance at Shasta, fully expecting her to be caught off guard, maybe protest at my being forward, but she isn't doing any of that. Instead, she's sitting there looking at Adelpha as if she was about to say the same thing.

An eternity passes before Adelpha clears her throat. "I suppose I owe you both that much. In truth, I've enjoyed getting to know the both of you so much that in a way, I was being selfish by not telling you what you really want to know. Your mother, Calliope, or Callie as you later knew her, was a wonderfully charming woman, full of passion and energy. She threw her whole self into an activity, though admittedly most of her activities were not any that I would have wanted for her." She takes a drink from her tea before continuing. "Music was her passion. She'd spend countless hours up in her bedroom listening to records, cassettes, CDs of musician after musician, her taste always evolving, though she typically listened to her favorites on repeat. Her taste in music was the complete opposite of mine. I was brought up on classical music, same as her father. So, when she spent hours blaring The Cure, well let's just say we were none too happy."

"So Mom got mad and left home because of your musical differences?" I ask.

"No dear, well, not in entirety. I loved your mother very much but we fought nonstop. Not just about our differences in music. Maybe it was because I expected more from her, or she just loved to fight, but we were never close. When your mother told me she was pregnant, I admit I was not happy. She was only twenty, unemployed, still in college. It broke her father's heart, her carelessness, but eventually, as the pregnancy progressed, we grew excited and looked forward to helping Calliope raise the baby."

"What about the father?" I ask. "Did you know the father? Was it a boyfriend?"

"This is probably where most of my unhappiness came from. Calliope claimed she didn't know who the father was."

"What about you, Shasta? Were you able to locate him?"

"Nope," she says, shaking her head. "It's like he doesn't exist. No results whatsoever."

"Shall I continue?" Adelpha says rubbing her temples, which I learned pretty quickly is a sign that she's getting tired.

"Sorry, Adelpha. Go ahead," I say.

"A week before you were scheduled to arrive, Shasta, Calliope informed us that she wasn't ready to become a parent, and so had made arrangements with an adoption agency. Of course, we tried to talk her out of it, but once Calliope had made up her mind about anything, there was never any changing it."

"So why did she leave? After giving me up for adoption, why did she leave home and never contact you again?" Shasta asks.

"She did leave, yes, but she never stopped contacting me."

"The postcards," I say, to which she nods.

"Postcards?" Shasta asks, confused.

"Mom sent postcards to Adelpha every few months for years, up until I was five or six."

"Okay, but why did she leave, Adelpha?" Shasta asks, a layer of irritation coating her voice.

"If I'm being honest, I really have no idea. I know our fights continued, and intensified. I suppose I'd never fully forgiven her for her choices, especially not her choice to give you up for adoption. She never admitted it, but I think it was just too painful for her to stick around. Though she swore she felt she made the right decision, something inside of her changed and I think the longer she stayed in San Francisco the longer she'd feel like she was drowning. That's what Mitch told us, anyway."

I look at Shasta for clarification, but she just shrugs. *Who the hell is Mitch?*

"Um Adelpha, who is Mitch?" Shasta asks.

"Mitch Ciapatta. He was Calliope's best friend"

I do a mental scan of all the pictures I looked at up in her room. If Mitch was her best friend, that'd mean he'd have been in at least half of the pictures, or at least the ones where she's not posing with various band members.

"Hang on a sec," I say and bolt upstairs to Mom's room. I scan the pictures taped to the mirror on her vanity. Sure enough, there are several pictures of my mom with the same dude. I snag one of the photos from high school graduation and rush downstairs where I thrust the picture at Adelpha with a little more force than I'd meant to.

"Is this Mitch Ciapa-whatever?" I ask.

She nods. "Yes, that's him."

"Do you think he'd know who Shasta's father is?"

She chews on her bottom lip for a second. "I suppose if anyone would know that answer, it would be him. He works down at Sal's auto, well he owns it, took it over from his father after his passing."

I look at Shasta, who is staring off into a corner of the room, eyebrows crunched together like she's deep in contemplation. I wonder if she's thinking what I'm thinking.

"Shasta, we should go talk to Mitch."

"I don't know, Maddie. I mean, if the DNA tests couldn't give me any information, what makes you think this Mitch character would know?"

"I don't know. But it's worth a shot. If anything, we can ask him about the day she left, maybe what her frame of mind was or whatever."

She's about to answer when the front door flies open followed by the angry footsteps of Erin and Leonard storming into the room.

I jump up and rush to her. "Erin, are you guys okay?"

She's a complete mess, her long hair spilling out of a hat, mascara streaked across her face and her nostrils are flaring.

"Nope. Not okay at all. My super-freak of a father found out I was with Leonard because SOMEONE walked out of the bathroom in just his towel even though I texted him that I was facetiming my dad, and my dad fuhreaked. Like, he used words on us that he only uses in the locker room. He said I have to get home asap. Uggg I'm so freaking pissed at him...who the hell are you?" She's looking at Shasta and Shasta looks like a deer in headlights, which is probably the best way to respond to an angry Erin. I walk over to stand next to Shasta and place my hand on her shoulder.

"Erin, this is Shasta Green. My sister."

Recognition hits her face like a dodgeball. "For real? OMG I'm so sorry. Hi, I'm Erin Whitney, Maddie's spastic best friend and this," she reaches over and yanks on Leonard's arm, pulling him forward, "is my boyfriend and Maddie's other best friend, Leonard."

"Hi, nice to meet you," Leonard says, extending his hand. Shasta chuckles and then stands up to shake his hand and then Erin's.

"It's nice to meet you both. Sorry to hear about your overprotective father. I have one of those too. I'm 28 and he still hovers."

Erin rolls her eyes. "He's just nuts. He needs to worry less about me and more about what his players do when they aren't practicing."

"When are you leaving, dear?" Adelpha says, still sitting in her chair.

"Dad says now. He's even calculated how long it will take for us to get back to Ashland if we stick to the speed limit, and if I'm not home by that exact time, I'm basically dead. So um, Mads, how fast do you think you can pack?"

Pack? I can't leave, not now. Not when I'm finally just starting to get answers. And I'd only just met Shasta. I'm not ready to go home. I walk over to Adelpha and kneel in front of her.

"Is there any way that I can stay?" I ask. She smiles and runs her hand down the side of my face which makes the hair on my spine stand up because this was a gesture my mom used to do every day.

"Stay for as long as you'd like," she says.

"But how will you get home?" Erin stammers. She doesn't want to go home and face her dad alone, and I totally get that. I've always been the buffer for whenever she and her dad fought, but she'd just have to face him alone this time.

"I don't know, fly, bus, call Rafe." I stand up and take hold of Erin's hands. "Erbear, I really need to stay a little longer. Adelpha told us about this guy who might be able to give us some info on my mom and Shasta's dad, so I think we're gonna go check him out."

She scrunches her face at me. "I don't know Maddie. I don't think it's a great idea for you to be questioning some rando by yourself."

"He's not a rando. He was my mom's best friend. And I won't be alone. I'll be with Shasta."

"And I have a concealed weapons permit, so like, try and do something," Shasta says, winking at me. Erin sighs before pulling me in for a hug.

"Fiiiine. Just be safe and make sure you call me every day."

"I will."

I help her and Leonard pack their bags, load up the car, and after hugs and more promises to be safe and call every day, they drive off and I go back inside where Adelpha has made chamomile tea. We drink it around the kitchen table, munching on sweet biscuits and talking. When Adelpha looks like she can't keep her eyelids open any longer, she kisses both of us on the head and then heads for her room. We clean up the dessert dishes, finalize our plans for going to see Mitch and crash for the night.

***

Sal's Garage is off Market Street next to a ginormous Greek cathedral. We have a few orthodox churches back in Oregon; there's a massive robin's egg blue church in Rogue River you can see off I-5, but it's a shed compared to the Annunciation Greek Orthodox Cathedral.

Everywhere I look there's a Mediterranean restaurant. Three places selling gyros are lined up in a row, and across the street from Sal's is one of those places the meat is shaved off right in front of you.

We pull up and park in one of the available spots, of which there are many. Doesn't look like Sal's Garage sees a lot of business. I'm wondering if it has anything to do with the fact that Sal Ciapatta, so Adelpha says, was of Italian descent, and this is a predominantly Greek part of town.

We head into the office where a pocket-sized woman sits behind a desk staring at a spreadsheet on the computer through thick frames. She glances at us and asks how we can be helped, but I can't respond because of her bug-eyes.

Shasta chuckles. "We're looking for someone named Mitch Ciapatta."

"He's in the garage, dears. Just go out the way you came in, hang a left. Boom. Garage. Oh, don't forget to duck."

"Thanks," Shasta says, grabbing my arm. Before we get to the door, I wiggle free and slide back up to the desk.

"Have you ever heard of Warby Parker?"

"Who's that dear? A rap singer? I don't like rap."

"Never mind. Thanks."

I follow Shasta out. She's grinning. "Seriously?"

I shrug my shoulders. "What? Don't pretend you weren't bugged out by her bug-eyes."

She rolls her eyes as we duck into a rust-colored garage. Two Nissans are up on blocks in the back, and a 1969 Cherry-red firebird is in the middle, hood propped up with a middle-aged man bent over it, his head lobbing up and down in time with the Metallica song pounding from an old boombox. Yup, a boombox, like right out of the '80's.

"Are you Mitch?" Shasta yells. He doesn't stop rocking out so I walk over to him and tap his shoulder.

"What the...!" He cranks his arm back and spins around, sending his wrench flying. Shasta and I back up and crouch down. When we look up, he's clutching his chest, and I'm hoping I didn't just give this poor man a heart-attack.

"Didn't anyone ever tell you not to sneak up on an old man?" He's wheezing, which tells me he's a smoker, and his belly pooches out over his low-hanging belt. He's got to be around the same age my mom was before she died, but the belly, the receding hairline, and the wrinkled forehead make him look a good five to ten years older. The only thing he has going for him is the dimple on his left cheek.

He pulls out a towel from his back pocket and swipes it across his forehead. "Can I help you ladies with something?"

"That depends," I say. "Are you Mitch?"

He arches his left eyebrow. "Who wants to know?"

"Does the name Callie Crane, I mean Calliope Costas ring a bell?"

He lowers his arched eyebrow and wipes his entire face with the towel. "Calliope Costas. Haven't heard that name in a decade, give or take."

"Are you Mitch?" I ask again.

He nods. "Yeah. I'm Mitch. And you are?"

"I'm Maddie Crane, and this is Shasta Green. Calliope Costas was our mother."

His eyes bulge and dart back and forth between me and Shasta, as if he's searching for recognition, some similarity to Mom to convince him we're not jerking his chain. Then his mouth eases into a smile.

"Well I'll be...yup. Y'all have her eyes."

When people say "well I'll be" after learning something, I feel like responding with "you'll be what?" It's stupid, but so is the antiquated figure of speech. What's wrong with "holy shit" or "no freaking way"? Packs a greater punch if you ask me.

"Wow." He rubs his stubbled chin, smearing grease from his hands. "I didn't even know she had children."

"You mean other than the one she gave up for adoption," I say.

He busts up. "I have a feeling you don't beat around the bush."

"Not if I can help it. I find whacking right through it yields better results."

"Come on. Let's go into my office. You guys want some coffee? It isn't great but it does the trick."

It couldn't be any worse than Rafe's. "Sure, I'll have a cup. Black, please."

He looks at Shasta. "No thanks. I'm good."

"Not a coffee drinker I take it."

She shakes her head. "Oh I drink coffee, but I'm gonna go out on a limb and guess that your coffee isn't French press or cold brew."

"I get it. You're one of those bougie coffee snobs. Should have guessed." He doesn't say it with any hint of snark. I could tell he was genuine. We sit down at two torn chairs by a desk and he hands me a chipped mug of coffee that smells like Folgers and tasted like how I imagine the inside of a garbage can could taste. I was mistaken. It could be worse than Rafe's.

"So tell me about Cal. How is she?"

Crap. He doesn't know. "Um, well she passed away earlier this year. Breast cancer."

"Oh hell. I'm so sorry. I didn't know. I haven't spoken to her in so long, her or her parents. Last time I even saw her folks was right before her dad died. Must have been fifteen-some-odd years ago."

"It's fine," I say. "I mean, it sucks but...yeah."

He runs a hand through the side of his hair. "Your mother. She sure was a spitfire back in the day. Caused her mom so much grief." He gets up and snatches a photograph off of a shelf and hands it to me. She and Mitch were standing outside a dive bar. She was wearing a white midriff that said "RELAX" under a blue and grey flannel shirt, cut-offs, and Doc Martens.

"This is us right after a Pearl Jam concert in 1990 up in Seattle. Of course, this was when they were known as Mookie Baylock. Cal swore they were gonna be huge. Turned out to be right."

I hand the photograph back to Mitch. "She looks so different."

"How so?"

"The Cal that I knew went by Callie, lived in yoga pants, camisoles and long sweaters, with crystals dangling from her neck. She also didn't listen to rock music. It was mostly drum circles and new age stuff."

"So she never went on tour with any rock bands?"

I scoff. "God no. Yoga guru's yes. Rock bands, no. I convinced her to see The Decemberists once, but that was only because they were playing the same venue as the Avett Brothers"

He chugs down the last bit of his coffee and wipes his mouth on his sleeve. "So, what brings you in here?"

I elbow Shasta in the arm. As curious as I am, this is something she needed to do.

"Well, we were wondering what you could tell us about her decision to give up her baby. Her mom said if anyone would know it would be you," Shasta asks.

He stares at her real hard before he says, "You're the baby, aren't you?"

"Yup. I'm the baby"

"Why didn't you ask her? Before she died?" he asks.

"Well because I didn't get a chance to meet her before she died. She agreed to a closed adoption and it wasn't until last year that I did one of those DNA tests. Since she changed her name, the closest I could get to was Adelpha, and she told me they hadn't been on speaking terms for over a decade."

He closes his eyes and runs a hand through his hair. I'm sure it isn't easy for him to hear all of this. First, we tell him this woman he used to be close with is dead, then we tell him she had kids. Adelpha said they were childhood best friends, but if they hadn't spoken in over a decade, now going on two really, because she's never mentioned this dude at all, how close were they?

"Adelpha said you and my mom were best friends?" I ask, picking at a corner of the desk. A sliver of wood sticks into my thumb under the nail and I wince, stick my thumb in my mouth to suck it out.

"In a manner of speaking. People gravitated around Cal like she was the Sun, and she made everyone feel like they were her best friend. But none of them ever knew her the way I did."

"Did you guys ever date?" I ask. He smiles and shakes his head.

"Nah, I adored her, but we weren't each other's type. She was a bit wild and I preferred the more reserved."

"How come you guys stopped talking? She never once mentioned you."

"It's complicated."

"So uncomplicate it. We're smart women."

He leans across his desk on his elbows and smirks, but not in a rude sort of way. I'm starting to gather that most of how this Mitch guy acts, the way he says things, probably could be taken as him being a jerk but that's totally not the vibe he gives off.

"The last time I heard from Cal, like really heard from her, she was about to leave for India to go to some yoga training or whatever with some people she met in Ashland. I thought she was crazy, she'd only known these people for like six months, but she was dead set on going, and when she came back three months later, I get a postcard from her, and all it said was *Life is beautiful. Namaste.* I tried to call her at the place she was staying but it was like she didn't want to be bothered."

"Were you angry?" Shasta asks. "How'd you take it? Basically, being blown off."

"Nah I wasn't angry. She left because she needed her space. If that meant from me as well, I wasn't going to deny her. I'm just real sorry I didn't try harder to get in touch. Time got the better hand. I met a girl, got married, got divorced, inherited this place. That's all there is."

"Do you know who Shasta's father is?" I ask.

He pulls his shoulders up to his ears, inhales, and then drops them down with his breath. "Nope. I don't. I don't know who he is."

"Mitch, you were her best friend. You're telling me you don't know who knocked her up? Was it a boyfriend?"

"She never had a boyfriend. Monogamy wasn't her thing. Always a series of boys coming and going"

Great. So basically, my mom was a tramp. What's that old-timey word? Floosy?

"You really have no idea?" I press.

He shakes his head hard. "No I don't, and the truth is neither did she."

"What do you mean?" Shasta asks.

"I mean what I said. She didn't know. Look, your mom was the coolest girl I knew but she was also pretty reckless. She was obsessed with her music and with following bands around and on the night this picture was taken," he holds up the photograph and waves it around, "she started hanging out with a group of roadies for the band that opened for Pearl Jam. She doesn't remember much of what happened other than there was drinking, and there was sex. The next two weeks she hopped from club to club to see The Cure, and four weeks later she was pregnant."

"Well. My origin story sucks." Shasta kneads her temples with her fingers. I have no idea what to say or even what to think. I knew my mom was a free spirit, all about love and freedom of expression, but she'd always taught me to respect myself and you know, not sleep around with a dozen men. What a hypocrite, right? She basically had an orgy with the roadies of all these different bands. I turn to Shasta. She looks shocked, and a little sick. I'm just glad she was adopted into a decent family.

Mitch sighs. "Look, I know it sucks and that probably wasn't the hopeful story you were expecting. She changed though, afterwards."

"How so?" I ask.

"She kinda shut down," he says. "The whole idea of being a mother freaked her out, and the fact that she had no idea who the father was didn't help. Then there was the guilt she got from her parents, especially her mom. She said every time her mom looked at her it felt almost like another layer of guilt was being added and it just got to be too much. So, when she'd made up her mind that she didn't want to keep the baby, I helped her find an adoption agency. We hoped that once the baby was born and with the new family, she'd be able to pick up the pieces and move on, figure out what kind of life she'd want to have, but instead all she felt was trapped. She wanted to leave, I gave her contact information for some relatives outside of Eugene, my dad gave her a car, and that was the last I saw her."

"She lived in Eugene before she ended up in Ashland?" I ask.

He shakes his head. "Nah, she never made it that far up the I-5. Fell in love with Ashland and this big group of hippies and that was it. Look, girls I'm sorry I can't be of any real help to you. I wish to hell I hadn't lost touch with her." He reaches across the table, taking hold of Shasta's hands.

"I'm extra sorry that you never got the chance to know her, honey. Your mom was a wonderful person and I know, had she been more mature and put together, she'd have been a good mother to you."

"Thanks Mitch." She squeezes his hands and pulls free. "Just so you know, I'm not like, broken or anything. I grew up with awesome parents. But still, thank you."

We say our good-byes and hop in the car to head back to Adelpha's. Shasta is silent the entire drive, and I don't know what to say. The Calliope that Mitch knew was not at all the Callie who raised me. They were two very night and day people, almost like a whole Invasion of the Body Snatchers case. I don't know which one Shasta would want to know about. I suppose she'd need to know both to get the full picture of this mother she never had. I should say something to her though, even if it sounds like gobbledygook. I'm the one that made her go see Mitch in the first place.

"I'm sorry Mitch didn't know who your father was."

She shrugs. "Yeah, it's alright. I went in assuming I'd get nothing anyway. Better than having my hopes let up."

"Still, it must suck knowing that you'll never find out who he was, and the fact that your biological mom slept around a whole bunch."

"It really doesn't bother me. Does it bother you? She's your mother too, I mean, she raised you and all."

I bite my lip. Should it bother me? It was in her past. Also, she was in her early 20's. Isn't that the time you're supposed to have lots of sex and get it all out of your system before you settle down with someone? After my dad left, my mom put all her attention into the yoga studio and me until she met Rafe, so as far as I know she only dated two men my whole life.

"It doesn't bother me that she slept around a whole bunch and made poor decisions when she was young. What bothers me is the fact that she lied about everything. I asked her point blank who her parents were and she said she didn't have any. I asked her what it was like growing up in San Francisco and she just said it was boring. I'm sorry, but from the pictures on her wall, the contents of her closet, and the stories from Mitch and Adelpha, she did not have a boring life."

"Maybe she was concerned you'd judge her," Shasta says.

"I guess, but at least she'd have been honest. She always used to tell me live truthfully, make an honest living but like, what a load of crap that was because she wasn't living an honest life."

"Yeah well sometimes shame can do that to a person."

"Do you think if you'd been raised in the system or had like shitty adoptive parents, you'd feel stronger about this?" I ask her. She takes zero time at all to reply.

"Oh without a doubt. I'm grateful that my adoptive parents are so awesome. I wish you could meet them. In fact...what would you think about coming to Calistoga with me? You can meet my family. My parents, my husband and daughter, and I'd really like you to meet my sister Caroline."

I don't answer right away. I've only just met Shasta. Is it too soon to then meet her entire adoptive family? As if she is reading my mind, Shasta says, "Look, Maddie, it's okay if you want to say no. I realize now it's kind of a lot asking you to meet my family, especially since you and I just met."

We pull up to Adelpha's. She opens the front door and steps out onto the porch holding a basket of what appears to be muffins. My mouth waters. I think about what my mom would want me to do, what she'd say. She embraced a whole group of people as her new family and even though she might have been scared, she did it anyway. I think about all she's gained from it, all the people who came in and out of our house, bellies full of food, spirits refreshed. She always said we needed to keep our hearts open, and I think she'd tell me to do just that right now.

"Sure, why not. Let's go meet your family."

June 8 1992

Dear Mama,

    I know it's been quite some time since you've heard from me. Don't worry I'm still alive. I tried to call once or twice once I came back from India but maybe you guys changed your number? Anyway, I'm writing to say that India was amazing. I learned so much about myself and how to be at peace with not just my inner self but with the world. I feel I can finally settle into the role I was meant to play. I'm a certified yoga instructor now, I teach classes at the wellsprings and at a studio here in town. Roxy and Michael have been so generous letting me rent out the apartment above their shop. I wish you could meet them. Some day. I hope you and Daddy aren't still holding out hope for my return. I really feel this is where I'm supposed to be. It may not be what you had wanted for me (I was so never going to become a doctor!) but everything just feels...aligned, you know? My love to you and Daddy. The divine light in me celebrates the divine light in you.

    Namaste, Callie.

Chapter Five

AFTER we say goodbye to Adelpha, making sure to promise I will call every other day, we hit the road. It's early. Since being down here in California I have become a morning person. If Mom could only see me now. I was late to class pretty much on a daily basis in middle school and high school because I refused to get out of bed. They really shouldn't have invented the snooze button, you know? When has it ever done anybody any good?

Adelpha packs us three days' worth of Eliopsomo, which is a delicious olive oil bread, thyme-honey, various meats and cheeses, and fruits, even though Calistoga is only about an hour and a half away.

"You never know when you might be hungry. Plus, there's traffic," she says, placing the basket in the backseat of the car before kissing me on the cheek. I'm instantly overcome with how sad I am to leave her, even though I know I'll be back in a few days. Strange, how you can miss a person you basically just met.

While we drive, I munch on the contents of the snack box while Shasta tells me about her crazy dorm room stories. It has become very evident that she's a big talker, but not like the kind of person who talks a bunch because they like the sound of their own voice. She seems like someone who loves the art of conversation and genuinely getting to know people. She's animated when she speaks, using her hands as she gesticulates, which doesn't seem entirely safe seeing as how she's the one driving.

As we get closer and closer to Calistoga, an uneasy feeling settles in my tummy and my palms sweat. I realize now I never asked her what she's told her family about me and my mom, and while she claims her family was cool with her reaching out to me, how cool are they actually?

"Ok so what should I expect from your family?" I ask, hoping she doesn't notice the nervousness in my voice.

"What do you mean?"

"I'm assuming you told them I was coming home with you, yeah?"

"Yeah, of course."

"Ok, so like, are they cool with meeting me so soon? Do they even actually want to meet me?"

She laughs. "Maddie, they are totally cool with meeting you. My parents are the nicest people on the planet. Trust me, they are excited to meet you. Same with my husband and daughter. You don't have anything to worry about."

"What about your sister Caroline?" I ask.

She hesitates before answering. "I think you'll like Caroline. At least, I hope you will. Sometimes she can be a little unapproachable, but she's got such a huge heart."

"Uh oh, what do you mean by unapproachable?"

"She's just...hard around the edges. She tends to judge right away, and sometimes that makes it hard for people to get to know her. But trust me, once they do, once she lets people in, she's fiercely loyal and cares deeply."

Yeah, I don't know if I want to meet someone who's gonna judge me hard core the second I step a foot out the car. Shasta looks at me and laughs.

"Dude, you look totally freaked out. It's not gonna be that bad. You'll like her, I promise."

I don't know how much faith I want to put into that promise. Even the way she says it doesn't sound convincing. I don't do well with the judgy girls. Normally I have Erin at my side to deal with them. I'm going to wind up saying something totally awkward and out of place, I just know it.

I've never cared before one way or another if anyone liked me but for some reason, and I have no idea why, she wasn't going to be anything to me other than my new sister's other sister(how completely unnatural does that sound?), but I wanted Caroline to like me. Maybe I'm just thinking that it's weird for both of us. I should care more about my actual sister liking me, if I'm going to care at all, but I can tell already that she does. I'm not tooting my own horn or anything, thinking *well I'm the shit so of course who wouldn't like me*. It's just in the way she smiles at me when we talk, how the past two days we've talked to each other in a level of comfort reserved only for people who really truly know each other. Like sisters.

We take the exit for Calistoga and drive another five miles into the country before hanging a left down a gravel road lined with olive trees shading the length of the road. We burst out into a clearing, the driveway leading up to a pale-yellow ranch style house with a wrap-around porch, and acres of grape vines off to the left.

"Holy crap. This is beautiful," I exclaim.

Shasta smiles at me as she pulls up to the porch, parks, kills the ignition.

"Bienvenidos a casa Green."

I unbuckle and get out of the car just as the door to the house is thrown open and a pint-size version of Shasta leaps off the porch and barrels into her. Shasta bends to scoop the little girl up into her arms and spins her around. Red pigtails flip around, loose strands sticking to whatever red is stuck to her face.

"Hello my little beans, I missed you so much!" Shasta sings, kissing the girl up and down her face. Once she's returned to the earth, she spots me looking at her and ducks behind her mother.

"Sarah honey, don't be shy. This is the girl I was telling you about. Do you remember?" The girl squeezes her tiny head in between Shasta's legs and stares up at me. Normal people would smile and wave, maybe say something nice like "I love your little pig-tails" or "hey there squirt" but there's something in her eyes, a mischievous twinkle, if you will, that tells me she'd prefer a less formal cheesy greeting, so instead I stick my tongue out at her. She beams, pushes herself all the way through Shasta's legs and tugs at the hem of her shirt.

"Mommy, I like her she's funny, what's her name again?"

"I'm Maddie. Maddie Crane. What's your name?"

"Sarah. Well it's Sarah-Jane Green, but I just like the Sarah. Not the Jane."

I laugh. "Alright then, Sarah it is."

"Do you like monster trucks? Because I like monster trucks. Auntie Caroline says I'm supposed to like dolls but I don't. I like monster trucks."

I look at Shasta who only offers a shoulder shrug. "Uh sure, I like monster trucks, what's not to like?" She's about to say more when the front door opens again and a heard of people spill out onto the stairs. There's an elderly couple who look to be in their late 60's I presume to be the parental figures. Behind them, a stocky Ed Sheeran look-a-like with thick black frame glasses, followed by a slender 20-something with strawberry-blonde hair swept over her shoulder into a braid. She comes to a lean against the top post of the porch, crossing her arms and settling her face into the worst case of RBF I've ever seen. Welp, so much for her liking me.

Shasta looks at me apologetically before sliding one hand into Sarah's, the other into mine and leading us to the porch. "Hey guys. Mom, Dad, I didn't expect you to be here. I said we'd come over after Maddie got settled."

The older woman pushes past her husband and Caroline, taking hold of the rail and coming down the stairs. She winces with each step, but she's got a hard face which tells me she can kick ass if she needs to.

"I know honey, but we were just too excited to wait." She hugs Shasta and then comes over to me, scooping my hands into hers and then pulling me into a hug. She's got some girth, and I fall right into her, collapsing in the full weight of the hug. It's the most in the way of comforting I've felt since before my mom got sick, and it's reminding me of how powerful a good hug can be. Not at all like the pity hugs I received at Mom's service. I feel like I could stand here all day buried in her arms, but she pulls away, holding me at shoulder's distance.

"You must be Maddie. Honey, we are so delighted to meet you," she says.

"Thank you. It's nice to meet you too."

Then she says, "oh my, Shasta you and Maddie look so much alike," and I know she's fibbing because aside from the eyes, we look nothing alike.

"Caroline, don't you think the resemblance is uncanny?"

Caroline shrugs her shoulders. "Not really Mom."

Oh how I wish Erin were here. Then Shasta's dad comes down the stairs, but instead of hugging me, he thrusts out his hand. I take it and we shake, after which he pulls his hand away and shakes it out.

"My, that's quite a grip you got there." Everyone is always surprised by my handshake. I guess they assume since I'm a girl that my grasp will be limp and weak, but I learned from Rafe that a handshake should be strong, firm, two swift shakes up and down before releasing.

"I get that a lot," I say. Caroline is still leaning on the porch. It's clear she has zero interest in joining the rest of her family in meeting me. WTF? I know I said ordinarily I don't care what people think of me, and that's generally true, but what *does* piss me off is when I'm disliked for no reason at all. Like if a person hasn't even met me and already acts like a Grade-A bitch, that is beyond frustrating to me. I don't care if it's weird or whatever that her sister has another sister, but show some class, is what I want to say. But I don't say that. Because I have class. So instead, I smile sweetly and look up at her and say, "hey you must be Caroline. It's good to meet you." She snickers but Shasta flicks her a warning glance, just as Stephen grabs her by the elbow and leads her down the stairs to join the rest of us. Stephen pulls Shasta in for a hug before turning to me and pulling me in for a hug. This family is really into hugs.

"Nice to meet you, Maddie. I'm Stephen." Up close he looks a lot older than 28, and a little less like Ed Sheeran, but more like Rupert Grint, though his hair is more a copper than than a deep red. When he smiles, his eyes disappear. I don't find either Ed Sheeran or Rupert Grint to be attractive by any standards. I've always been more a Tom Felton fan myself, but he's wearing a Bob's Burger's t-shirt, grey chucks, and ripped-knee jeans, and seems quirky enough that I can see why Shasta gravitated towards him.

"Well I hope you're hungry," Mr. Green says. "Mrs. Green whipped up a mean quiche. I hope you like ham. Oh, and eggs." He's already turned towards the porch before I can answer. Good thing I love both ham and eggs.

We eat lunch, an amazing spread of quiche, toast with homemade jam, sticky buns, bowls of fresh fruit, and copious amounts of coffee. Mr. and Mrs. Green fill me in on any details Shasta left out about her childhood, which was basically all the embarrassing stuff, and Stephen rambles on and on about what Shasta was like in college (not quite studious more rebellious) and Sarah sits on my lap the whole time, occasionally jumping off to retrieve a car from her bedroom to show me. Every time she moves her little pigtails whip me in the face and I can't get over how she smells like cupcakes and Play Dough, which is weird because neither item is anywhere within eyesight, unless she's got a secret stash in her pockets. Ordinarily, I don't like spending this much time around little kids, like I said, I've never been great with them, but there's something about Sarah that makes me forget all about that. She's only five but she's already so witty and smart, and she knows a surprising amount about monster trucks that I wasn't aware five-year-old girls would know. That's what I get for making gender-assumptions.

Every now and then I catch Caroline looking at us from her side of the table, glaring so deep you'd think someone was shining a light directly into her eyes. She's stunning, I'll admit, but jealousy is an ugly color on her.

By the time Shasta's family leaves, it's early evening. None of us are hungry for any form of a dinner since we basically stuffed ourselves all afternoon, so I say I'm beat and Shasta shows me to the guestroom slash design studio. In one corner is a four-poster metal frame queen size bed with a mint green and cream comforter, a nightstand, and an old rustic armoire. In the other side of the room is a headless mannequin that will be sure to give me nightmares, a sewing desk with a baby blue sewing machine, a rack with several spools of thread sticking out, and bolts of fabric propped up in a corner.

"Sorry about the mess," Shasta says, scooping up armfuls of loose fabric and cramming them into a drawer by the sewing desk. "I'm normally a pretty neat and clean person, with the exception of this room. I can't for the life of me keep it tidy."

"It's alright, really this isn't that bad. You should see Rafe's painting room in the back of our house. It always looks like tubes of paint have exploded, and brushes are everywhere. I'm used to it."

"I know the house looks big from the outside, but really, it's just three bedrooms. Not enough space for a guest room and a sewing room." She ducks out into the hall and returns with two towels and a wash cloth. "So, the bathroom is down the hall, last door on the left. Sometimes Sarah gets up in the middle of the night so if you hear someone walking around it's probably her." I take the towels from her and set them on the bed. "Thanks again for coming up, Maddie. It really means a lot."

"Yeah no problem. Everyone seems nice. Well, almost everyone."

"Don't worry about Caroline. I promise she won't be mean forever." I don't believe her, but I just nod and say goodnight. After she leaves, I pull my phone out from my bag and call Erin. She picks up on the first ring.

"Maddie! You're alive."

"Of course I'm alive. Why wouldn't I be?"

"Oh, I don't know, maybe because you drove up to God knows where with someone you barely know to meet strange people."

I roll my eyes. "Erin, I drove an hour and a half away. It's not like *Deliverance* or anything."

She sighs. "Fiiiine. So, how's the family? Are they nice?"

"Mostly"

"Mostly?" she asks

"Her parents are super adorable. They're in their 60's and live down the street on an alpaca farm if you can believe it."

"What about the husband and the daughter?" she asks.

"Husband is cool. He's super nerdy but in a cool way, has a wicked sense of humor. Sarah, the daughter, is probably the neatest kid I've ever met."

"For real?" she laughs. She's well aware of my aversion to small children.

"Yeah I don't know what it is. She's just neat."

"And Caroline? The other sister? How is she."

I chip at the polish on my nails. "She's already made up her mind to hate me."

"What do you mean?" I can hear in her voice the low growl she gets when she's about to become overprotective.

"Well for starters she refused to even say hi to me when we were introduced, and then she kept glaring at me all day while I was with Sarah. I don't know what Shasta said about me before we met, but it's plain as day that she doesn't like me."

"What a bitch. I knew I should have told my dad to eff off so I could come with you. I mean, who does this girl think she is?" I need to diffuse the situation before she really starts to rage.

"Erin. Calm down, it's okay. Contrary to popular belief, I can handle a mean girl all by myself. I don't need you to beat her up for me."

She sucks in a few gulps of hair. "Fine whatever. You just better let me know if she does or says anything to you."

"What are you going to do? Drive down her and kick her ass?"

"You're damn right I will!" So much for diffusing.

"Change of subject. How was your dad when you got home? Did you make it in time?"

"Uggg barely," she grumbles. "He was sitting on the porch when I got home and didn't even wait until we were inside the damn house before he laid into me. Mrs. Larkin across the street had to come over and tell him to stop yelling at me, then he told her to mind her own beeswax. It was awful."

"What did he say about Leonard? Are you super grounded?"

"Yup. He said I can't see Leonard at all for the rest of the summer. Like, hello! I'm an adult but do you think he gives a crap? Nope. He has his stupid football players following me around like creepy stalkers, reporting back my every move to Dad. He is being so freaking ridiculous. Does he not know that he can't control who I am with when I go to college? He can't stop Leonard from seeing me at U of O. "

"What's Leonard think about it?"

"He's being chill about it. Thankfully he knows the level of psycho my dad is. Roxy sneaks him into the store sometimes so I can see him on my lunch breaks."

"Sorry your dad's so bananas." I want to be as pissed as she is, but the truth is, at least her dad was around and cared. If I had a boyfriend I spent entirely too much time with, I'm sure my dad wouldn't even notice, because to notice, you'd have to actually be around.

"So, what's happening while you're in Calistoga?" Erin asks.

"Um not sure. I think Shasta wants to show me the family business. Beyond that I don't know. I'm gonna go shower now though and sleep. Today was super exhausting."

We say goodbye and after I shower, I bury myself under the comforter and fall asleep.

February 8 1993

Mama,

I know you're upset I didn't make it to Daddy's funeral. I don't expect you to understand my reasons for not being there. Please think about coming up to the wellsprings.

Namaste, Callie

Chapter Six

WHEN I wake in the morning, it isn't by the pleasant chirping of birds outside the window, or from the aroma of a good strong pot of coffee, or even by a rooster's call, which you would expect since this is basically the country. Nope. It's by twenty-five pounds of small child jumping full force onto my chest while singing, "time to wake up!" followed by a behemoth golden retriever jumping onto my legs. Then Shasta runs in, waving a spatula at the dog and scooping Sarah up off my chest.

"I am so sorry, Maddie! I told Sarah to wait until you woke up on your own."

I sit up and yank my hair out of its bun. "It's totally fine. Can't think of a better way to be woken up. But um-" I point at the beast sitting outside the door- "what the heck is that?" I'd at first thought it was a golden retriever, but now that my glasses are on and I can get a proper look at it, I have no idea what breed it is. It's massive like a great dane or a mastiff, but furry and fluffy like a blown-dry golden retriever.

"Oh him? That's Archie. We got him right before Sarah was born. He's a new-fie-mastiff. Total sweet-heart." I stick my hand out towards him and he lumbers over, runs his hot thick tongue across my hand and then up my arm before resting his head on the bed.

"Awe I think he likes you."

"Awesome." I rub my arm and hand across the comforter. "Gross."

"You get used to it. So listen, Stephen wants to take you on a tour of the vineyards if you're up for it."

"Sure sounds like fun." Admittedly, touring a vineyard did not sound like fun. The thing is, I don't like wine. Actually, I don't really like the taste of alcohol at all, and I know what you're thinking, *"Maddie, you're only 18, not at all of legal age to drink, how can you even know what alcohol tastes like?"* and to that I say puhlease. Every teenager has tasted alcohol before they're 21 either by sipping from their parents' wine glass, swiping a bottle of whatever is most convenient from their parents' pantry, or chugging a beer at a party, most likely purchased by an older sibling. It's just what teens do, and any teen that says they haven't tried at least the teensiest sip, is lying.

I don't tell any of this to Shasta though, that I have zero interest in touring her vineyard, but I did come here to see what she does for a living, to be a part of her life, get to know her and her family. Since owning and running a vineyard is a big chunk of her life, I should show interest.

We eat a breakfast bigger than yesterday's lunch and then I follow Shasta and Sarah to the garage where we pile into a golf cart (yes an actual golf cart!) and motor on down the dirt road behind their house about two miles until we arrive at another house similar to theirs, which I am told is their "work house". One of my guilty pleasures when I have down time is to watch all the cooking shows on The Food Network, so *Worst Cooks in America*, *Farmhouse Rules*, *The Pioneer woman*, etc etc. Anyway, if you've ever seen *The Pioneer Woman*, you know they own a cattle ranch, and Ree (I feel I can call her that. I've seen enough of her shows that I feel we're besties) does all of her production videos from their lodge, which is their guest house slash work house, and is separate from where they actually live. This is how I think of where we are. There's a wrap-around porch, identical to the one at Shasta's actual house, a beautiful array of zinnias planted in flower beds lining the walkway to the house, and a play structure to the left where Sarah bolts to upon exiting the golf cart. Behind the house and stretching out for miles up and down the hills is a sea of luscious green vines. The sun, already high in the sky, is hot on my skin, but thankfully there's a breeze, and with it a sweet crisp scent of something I can't quite put my finger on.

Shasta comes to stand next to me, slings an arm around my shoulder. Today she's wearing red plaid capri's, a black vintage t-shirt with a picture of The Rolling Stones, and combat boots. Her hair is in a messy bun and it's only now I realize that the back of her hair, right around the nape of her neck is shaved.

"Well, what do you think?" She's looking off into the distance at the rolling hills.

"It's awesome. I mean, we have loads of vineyards back in Ashland, but this is the first one I've seen, you know, up close and personal. How big is your vineyard?"

"Um, somewhere around 29 acres. We're nowhere near the largest in the valley, but at the same time we're not the smallest."

"Are there others that just grow the vines as opposed to being vineyards and wineries?" Look at me, I guess I had more interest than I thought.

"For sure." She smiles at me and pulls me toward the porch, beckoning for Sarah to follow us.

"I'll take you out to the vines, that's where I spend most of my time, but first I'll show you around the office."

It's the most lavish office I've ever seen. There's a sitting room with two chocolate leather couches and a coffee table; various wine related magazines are lined up in neat rows across it. The walls are pale yellow with pictures of grapes, vines, and bottles of wine from Stollhouse Winery and Vintage Cellars, the two wineries who hold contracts with Sweet Briar Cellars.

A set of French doors lead into Stephen's office. There are two desks, each hooked up with a double monitor situation, and behind one of them sits a slender guy, I'd say somewhere in his thirties, metal frame glasses pushed up onto his head. When he sees us walk in, he cracks a perfectly symmetrical smile, pushes away from the desk and comes to meet us. As he steps around the desk, I see he's wearing a baby blue button-down shirt, cuffed khaki pants, and what I'm pretty sure are snake skin loafers. Oh, and he's also got an ascot around his neck.

"O.M.G you must be Maddie, Shasta's long-lost sister! Hello I'm Kendall. It's so great to meet you." He sounds exactly as I expected him to sound. His voice is high and sing-songy, like the dude in that Reece Witherspoon movie who says *"oh my gosh the bend and snap! Works every time."* I'm not too keen on him calling me the "long lost sister" but whatever. He sticks his hand out for a shake and when I grasp it, he keeps all of his fingers erect, so it's basically the weakest handshake in the world, but his smile is nice and his eyes sparkle, so I figure I won't hold it against him.

"Kendall is our assistant. The eyes and ears of the vineyard. He basically runs this place," Shasta says. Kendall winks at me before returning to his desk.

"You gonna take her on the grand tour?" he asks, sweeping his arm out in the direction of the vineyards.

"Yup, that's the plan. Stephen took the cart down there already so I think we'll take the bikes. Can you have them brought around?"

"I'm on it. Have a good tour, Maddie. It was lovely to meet you." He jumps up and sashays out the back, pulling his phone out of his pocket as he goes and starts up an animated conversation with someone on the other end. He reminds me so much of Michael and Roxy's nephew it's not even funny. Like, from the sound of his voice to the way he commands the room, he's a carbon copy of Alex. I tug my phone out of my pocket and shoot a quick text to Erin while Shasta is talking with Sarah, who's just ran in from the play structure. I tell her about Kendall and she texts back, *what? No way you MUST take a pic!* Yeah fat chance because I know she'll show it to Alex and he'll have some words to say about it when I get back. One thing about Alex, he's absolutely, positively sure of himself and hates to be compared to anyone else, even if it's in the sincerest way. Like if I said *"omg Alex you look just like Chris Pine"* who by the way should be on People's Sexiest Man cover every single year, he'd freak out and tick off on his fingers all the ways that comparison was offensive, even though I also know he's got a major crush on Chris Pine.

I hear a what sounds like the *swoosh* from an aerosol can and look over to where Shasta and Sarah are sitting. Shasta is holding something up to Sarah's mouth and after counting down, presses the top of the cannister with her finger, and I recognize it as an inhaler just about the same time Shasta looks at me and says, "Sarah has asthma. I just need to tend to her for a sec."

I sit in one of the squishy leather couches and pretend to be busy on my phone. When Shasta has sufficiently fussed over Sarah and sent her off with the nanny, she slumps into the seat next to me.

"Everything okay?" I ask. Shasta's face is pinched and she looks a little pale but she quickly shakes it off and smiles.

"Oh yeah everything's fine. Sometimes her asthma acts up when she gets too active outside. She just started a new medication so it's been a little crazy. You ready to take a tour of the vineyards?"

I nod, pull myself up out of the couch before it has the chance to suck me all the way in and follow Shasta out the front where two bikes are waiting for us on kickstands. They are both bright purple with yellow handlebars and matching yellow banana seats. You heard. Banana seats, which I didn't even know they still made. In the front attached to the handle bars are wicker baskets and yes, even a bell. *Brrring! Brrring!*

"Hey Shasta, 1990 called. They want their banana seat bikes back."

She tilts her head and smiles. "You're hilarious. I happen to love these bikes. I found them at a flea market in Encino and they are the greatest things ever."

I take her word for it, strap on the helmet dangling from the handlebars, swing my leg over the seat of the bike and kick off, following her down the dirt road. It's only about a half of a mile, but biking between the groves with the morning breeze flowing through our hair feels awesome. I never spent any great amount of time as a kid on a bike. I mean, I obviously learned how to ride and in elementary school it was my preferred mode of transportation, but everywhere Erin and I went in Ashland was in walking distance, and if it wasn't, I drove us in my moms car. Riding next to Shasta, weaving back and forth, laughing, watching her spread her arms wide and close her eyes as she glides, for a moment I get an idea of what it would have been like growing up with a sister, and it makes me wish I'd ridden bikes with Mom more often since she rode her bike everywhere.

"Do you like riding bikes?" I ask Shasta as we pull up next to the golf cart, kick down the kickstand on our bikes and hang our helmets.

"I do, actually. My parent's farm is just down the road and Stephen's parents have a distillery a mile in the opposite direction and we usually, well, mostly me, Stephen isn't so much a bike person, but I like to ride my bike there."

"My mom...our mom loved to ride bikes too."

She spreads a mile across her face. "Oh yeah?"

"Yup. Since we live so close to her studio, she normally took her bike to work and to the co-op. Sometimes she even biked to Wellsprings which is like five miles from our house."

"That's cool. Thank you for sharing it with me." She squeezes my shoulder and starts walking. She wants to know more about Mom, I can tell, but it also seems like she's giving me the time and space needed to dole out information in small increments, allowing time to feel comfortable with her.

We find Stephen standing in front of a vine speaking in perfect Spanish to a guy who nods, committing to memory whatever is being discussed. When they've finished their discussion, the guy nods at us and disappears into the row of vines.

"Hello, ladies. Fancy meeting you here," Stephen says, arching his thick eyebrows up and down, which just makes his glasses slide down the bridge of his nose. Shasta flicks her thumb in the direction of the guy.

"What was up with Hector? Everything okay?" Before Stephen can answer, Shasta explains that while she's the vineyard manager, Hector supervises the migrant workers and has been with the family since he was fifteen.

"He wanted to talk about harvest season and what it's going to look like, where we're doing great and where we could be doing better. Come on, Maddie, I'll show you around the vines."

We meander through the many rows of the vineyard, stopping a few times so that Stephen can show me the vines which will grow Pinot Noir and Merlot, feel the soil, and tell me how the vines are planted. He may handle the business end, but he knows just as much about the agriculture as Shasta.

"Within the first couple of years, we try to make sure the vines don't produce any fruit at all," he says.

"Doesn't that seem kinda counterproductive? I mean, why plant something with the intention of producing fruit and then restrict it from doing just that?" I ask.

"I know it seems super weird, but you wanna make sure the vines are strong enough to support fruit so they need a full season, sometimes two, to just grow and get strong.

Then he tells me about the importance of pruning. Since it's June, and pruning typically takes place in March or April, there aren't vines left to prune, so instead he leads me to a section of vines where the grapes aren't quite ripening and shows me how to pinch back the foliage to allow for more sunlight. I start to wonder if maybe in another life he wasn't a teacher because for the next ten to fifteen minutes he gives me the history of Calistoga and all of wine country, what makes Calistoga such a great place to grow grapes-high elevation, the sloping hills, the ration of direct sunlight to evening wind, the soil that comes from the Russian River. All the while Shasta watches with a little smile on her face, in awe of her husband. It's annoyingly cute.

By the end of the lecture, and I say lecture because that's exactly what if felt like, I know more about the lifecycle of a grape, the vine it grew on, and how to harvest than I ever thought I would care to know. I actually found it super interesting though. I mean, I don't like the taste, and I don't really have any plans to farm anything, but just having the knowledge of where something is coming from is kind of cool.

"Do you guys get a discount on the wine from the places you grow for?" It's late evening and we're having dinner on the back porch. Stephen, who is also a phenomenal cook, grilled salmon and served it on a bed of mixed greens. It's a light dinner in comparison to the mounds of Greek food Adelpha's stuffed into my mouth every night, and the smorgasbord from yesterday's lunch.

"Well, it's kind of complicated," Shasta says, looking at Stephen.

"Complicated how?" I ask.

"Daddy and his brother don't get along," Sarah pipes up from across the table. She's impaling peas onto the teeth of her fork.

"Huh?" I ask, totally confused as to what Stephen's relationship with his brother has to do with wine.

"Vintage Cellars is owned by my brother Paul. Before him it was owned by my parents, same as Sweet Briar Cellars. Back then, this place did grow the vines and make the wine. There's a large shed on the other side of the property where the wine would be bottled and stored. Now we use it to store equipment. When my parents expressed their desire to retire, my brother and I couldn't agree on running the business together. I was more interested in the vines and he was more interested in furthering the winery, I mean he'd even studied to be a sommelier in France for a while."

"That's a thing? Like a thing you go to school for?"

"Oh yeah, it's a huge thing and Paul is actually really good at it. Anyway, we fought and fought, which wasn't all that surprising since my brother and I have never gotten along, and so finally my parents split the companies. They gave the winery to Paul and the vineyard to me with the understanding that we would continue to grow the grapes for Vintage Cellars. So, we grow the grapes and when they're ready we haul them over to Paul, and that's it. We try not to communicate with one another unless we need to, and it's usually through the family attorney."

"Yikes. That's intense. Must make family holidays fun."

"Well lucky for my family we never celebrated holidays. Jehovah's Witness. I'm not anymore, but Paul and his family and my parents are."

There were about a handful of Jehovah's Witnesses at my school growing up and they always had to be excused from class anytime we were going to celebrate a birthday, or have a holiday party. I always felt so bad for them because they had to miss out on all the festivities because of the religion their parents passed down to them. I mean, whatever, I get that people are entitled to practice whatever religion, but I still felt it was a bummer to not celebrate a birthday or Thanksgiving or even Christmas.

"He does have one thing going for him though." Stephen slides his fork into his fish and pops the bite in his mouth. "He's got a real soft spot for Sarah. Paul and his wife can't have kids of their own, so he kinda spoils Sarah rotten."

"I like Uncle Paul," Sarah says with her mouth full of peas, legs swinging so fast under the table I get kicked a few times. "He buys me ice cream and takes me to the movies."

"So what are the chances you guys will bury the hatchet?" I ask. He clicks his tongue a few times and then looks at Sarah, his eyes softening a bit.

"I don't know. I mean, I know that we should, not just for Sarah, but for my parents; they're old and won't be around forever, but there's just too much history."

This seems to be a growing trend, I'm noticing. Too much history between people to bury the hatchet. We have Stephen and his brother Paul, and my mother and grandmother. From what Adelpha told me, they tried and tried to get along but something always kept them from just getting over their beef and moving on. Even Erin and Maris go through phases where they have epic fights and shut each other out, but they usually resolve it quickly. Erin and I sometimes fight like sisters. Does that count? I remember one time in middle school our families took a daytrip to the Applegate and we set off down a lazy part of the river on innertubes. I don't know what the fight was over exactly but I remember Erin flipping my tube, I got pissed and while we were walking back to our parents she tried to apologize, but I was being a punk and wouldn't accept it. That just made her mad and we didn't talk for a week. That was hard for me, because I'd never gone that long without talking to her, so I packed up some of my most prized possessions, just random little trinkets really, and left them in a box on her porch with an apology note.

After dinner Sarah wants me to go to the porch with her to look at her rock collection, so while Shasta and Stephen clean up the dishes and package the leftovers, I sit cross-legged on a porch pillow and listen to Sarah talk about her rocks. She's not only telling me where she got them, or who gave them to her, but she's also telling me the type of rock they are, *this one from Grandma Green is igneous and did you know igneous rocks are formed when hot molten rocks crystalize and solidifies, this sharp one is a quartzite my dad got for me in Canada. Sometimes it's used in road construction when it's all crushed.* I listen to her ramble on and on and I can't help but think she's probably the smartest five-year-old I've ever met. Now, that's not to say I've met or interacted with many five-year old's, but I've spent enough time hanging out around Leonard's little sisters to know a smart egg when I see one. Sarah is one smart egg. Not only that but she's also fun to be around. Normally I clam up around little kids, but after we look at all her rocks, she slides over the box with her monster trucks and we play with those for a good half hour, not once with me checking my phone for the time or to get on the internet.

"You're fun, Maddie," she says to me, driving Grave Digger up the bend of my leg and launching him off my knee. "Aunt Caroline doesn't like to play monster trucks with me."

"Well, she is an adult."

"Aren't you an adult?" she asks.

"I guess technically. But I'm still a teenager."

"How old are you anyway?"

I laugh. "I'm eighteen."

"I can count to eighteen. Probably even higher. Actually, I can count to fifty. Wanna hear?"

And so she counts, stretching out the word 49 and singing out 50 triumphantly, then takes a bow. I clap and whistle. "Rock on girlfriend, that's awesome."

She smiles up at me and it's the kind of smile that takes up her whole face, which is already so small to begin with. There's a dimple on her left cheek I didn't notice before.

After Shasta comes out to retrieve Sarah for bed, I stay out a little while longer on the porch swing, using the tips of my toes to rock back and forth. I send a few check-in emails from my phone, one to William Crawley (because he hates phone calls and would rather use the art of the written word to express sentiments), and one to my British grandparents who are still slightly peeved I opted not to spend my summer with them in London, even though I never even told them there was a distinct possibility that I would go over there. Also, like I said, I've only met them a handful of times, maybe four if I'm really keeping count. Also, their house, the one time I was there, smelled like wet dog and dirty socks. Oh, and the food was horrible. Beans for breakfast? Gross.

Once the emails are out of the way, I call Rafe, because he finds texts and emails too impersonal, and fill him in on my past few days. I can hear him say "uh huh" and "mmh-mm" as I tell him about Shasta's parents, her fun-loving husband, about her daughter (at this point he laughs because he's well aware of my awkwardness around children) and about how rude in general Caroline is, but when I get to talking about the vineyard and the rolling hills, he starts in on the questions, *how green are the hills? What do they look like in the early morning sun? how about as the sun sets? Do you have pictures of the vines?* and I know that he's trying to capture a mental image to use for one of his paintings. If there's one thing Rafe loves to paint more than anything in the world, more than his odd, funky shapes, and his Picasso throw backs, it's a mean landscape, only his landscape paintings aren't anything you'd expect, nothing they'd hang in hotels anyway. He puts a sort of Goya twist on it which makes them look both serene and creepy at the same time.

After I promise to take a crap ton of pics and upload them into our shared Google drive, I hang up and head inside. Shasta is curled up on the couch in the living room with Archie watching *Housewives* of some suburban town, and Stephen is sitting on a plush floor pillow with a gargantuous gaming PC on his lap, headphones cupping his ears, mumbling inaudibly. I look at Shasta and flick my thumb over to Stephen. She looks up at me and rolls her eyes.

"Marvel Ultimate Alliance 3 or something like that. We each have our thing. He plays video games I watch trashy tv."

I sit next to her on the couch, Archie stretching out his massive back legs across my lap, and watch tv with her until Stephen goes to bed and she decides we can't watch any more *Housewives* drama without copious amounts of double fudge ice cream. I don't say no to that. She returns from the kitchen with a carton and two spoons and while we overindulge, we gossip, almost as if picking up where we left off at Adelpha's. This time most of the conversation is directed at me, more in the form of rapid-fire questions: did I have a boyfriend (no), have I ever had a boyfriend (ugg, yes) have I ever had sex (um yeah I'm not answering that) (because the answer is no) am I excited to go to college eventually (undecided) who is my celebrity crush (Timothee Chalamet duh), have I ever snuck into a movie (who hasn't). By the time Shasta has run out of questions, it's after midnight. Neither of us can keep our eyelids open for much longer, so we say goodnight and I drag myself up the stairs and fall into bed.

I wake up the next morning with something on my chest again.

"Peek-a-boo, I see you!" Sarah giggles, yanking at the blanket covering my face. She smells like maple syrup and strawberries.

"I see you too," I say, rolling over until she rolls off me. I hope she didn't leave sticky syrup all over my blanket "What time is it?"

"You know I can't tell time yet, I'm only five."

"You mean you know everything in the world there is to know about rocks and trucks, but you can't tell the time? You're letting me down, kid." She tilts her head back and laughs, and for a second, I can see just a hint of Callie Crane in her smile.

"Is your mom up?" I ask.

"Yup. She's downstairs with Daddy punching herself in the face with caffeine."

I'm pretty sure I know what she means, but it sounds so ridiculous and strange coming from her because she so clearly doesn't know what it means. She shrugs her shoulders, flips off the bed and dashes out the door yelling, "last one downstairs is a stinky hamster!" Stinky hamster must be the new 'rotten egg' I guess.

When I get downstairs, Shasta is sitting at the table with a tablet in one hand and a mug of coffee in the other. Her mug says Dunder Mifflin Paper Company and when she looks up at me, we both bust up because my shirt says Schrute Beet Farms.

"Of course, you like *The Office*," she says, raising her mug up at me.

"Who doesn't?" I lower down into the chair next to her as Stephen slides a plate of steaming scrambled eggs in front of me followed by a mug of coffee.

"You liked scrambled, right?" he asks.

"Yup," I say woofing down a bite, my taste buds dancing spastically on my tongue. "OMG did you use milk and gruyere cheese?"

Stephen stretches a smile across his face, so wide he sort of looks like the Joker. You'd have thought I just told him he won the lottery.

Shasta chuckles. "See babe, told you she'd love your eggs. Everyone does."

I take another bite. "What's not to love? These are freaking amazing." I finish off the eggs in like a second and practically lick the plate clean before rising it and putting it in the dishwasher. I sit back down at the table and take a long slow drink from my coffee when the front door is thrown open and Caroline bounds through, tossing her purse onto the couch. Behind her trails a tall muscular guy I'd say is somewhere near 22 in a baby blue polo shirt, khaki cargo shorts, and flip flops. I think unless you live on the beaches of southern California and you surf regularly, as a dude, there's no real reason to wear flip flops. At least he isnt' wearing jeans and flip flops. That's just, well, I don't even need to go there. Anyway, he's got wavy sandy-blonde hair that frames his face, and I notice right away that one eye is brown and the other an emerald green. He is, by definition, what Erin would call "a major hottie". They linger in the living room to talk with Sarah for a few minutes before coming into the kitchen. Caroline leans in the doorframe while the major hottie goes to greet Stephen with a handshake and Shasta with a bear hug. Then he walks over to me and extends his hand.

"Hey how ya doing? I'm Caleb, Caroline's friend. You must be Maddie?"

"Guilty as charged," I say, setting down my coffee mug and shaking his hand. He looks back and forth between me and Shasta several times and then says, "man, you guys don't really look too much alike, except for in the eyes, and a little in the smile."

I can tell he's expecting me to say something like, *"what do you mean? Of course we look alike. Are you blind? The resemblance is uncanny"* but I'm not gonna. I already know that as I continue to meet the various people in Shasta's life, I'll be told how much we don't look alike, but it's already starting to get old. So instead, I shrug my shoulders and say, "I guess the genes are just stronger on my dad's side."

"So how long are you in town?" He pulls out a chair, flips it around and straddles it. I have no clue. One day? Two weeks? We never really discussed the duration before I climbed into Shasta's car.

"Um well, I'm kinda just flying by the seat of my pants here. No real end date or anything."

Caroline finally pushes off the wall, like she no longer needs to hold it up and slips into the seat next to Caleb. "Where are you from again?" she asks. There's a catch in her voice like she's asking not because she's genuinely curious but because what she'd like to do is send me back there asap.

"Ashland, Oregon," I say.

"Oh yeah, that's right. Home of...well what is it famous for?"

"It's not really famous for anything really. There's a Shakespeare festival every year, and an awesome independent film festival, but otherwise mostly old retired hippies and college kids."

Caroline's left eyebrow raises up ever so slightly. "So, your mom gave Shasta up and then ran off from the bay area to go live in some small Oregon town full of old retired hippies and college kids?" she says.

Caleb sucks in a breath and Shasta shoots a glare and must have kicked Caroline from under the table because the table shakes and then Caroline is grabbing at her shin.

"Caroline, what the hell?" Shasta asks.

Caroline shrugs her shoulders. "What? It was just a question."

"You know it wasn't *just* a question. Nothing is ever *just* anything with you."

"It's cool," I say, waving my hands at them. "I'm sure she didn't mean anything by it. Yes, it appears that is apparently what my mom did. But my mom was just some lady who gave birth to Shasta. Mrs. Callahan is her mother." I don't even know why I'm saying any of this, why I'm trying to be nice and placate everything. This chic wants to flick me shit because she's jealous or whatever and I know Erin would tell me not to take it, but that's why she's Erin and I'm me. Her balls have always been much bigger than mine.

Caroline rolls her eyes but then smiles, and it's the kind of smile that has zero amount of nice behind it, the kind that mean girls wear right before they are about to do something bitchy.

"So Shasta," Caroline says, shifting in her seat to look at Shasta. "I know Maddie is here to get to know you and all, but I was thinking maybe she could chill with me and Caleb today."

"For real?" Shasta asks, arching an eyebrow.

"Yeah I mean, I'm sure you have some work to catch up on and you probably want to spend time with Sarah."

"I'm actually caught up on work."

"Okay well how about I just want to get to know Maddie since we'll both be sharing you as a sister."

"Funny, you didn't seem to want to get to know me when we first met," I say.

She shrugs her shoulders. "I know and all I can say is sometimes I'm a bitch. Go ahead Caleb, tell her."

Stephen coughs from the sink. "Don't do it Caleb, it's a trap."

"I heard that Stephen," Caroline says, glaring. Caleb slides out of his chair and whips his phone out from his back pocket.

"I just remembered I have to make a phone call. Be right back." He all but runs out of the kitchen.

"Anyway," Caroline says, "Maddie will you please at the very least just come shopping with us and then out to lunch?"

I should say no. I mean, this girl absolutely can't be trusted. There's an angle she's trying to play and I'm 99 percent positive that if I say yes, I'm going to wind up the butt of some stupid joke, but she's sitting here smiling, and Shasta looks confused but also a little hopeful. So, I say, "yeah sure, why not."

Stephen and Shasta share a look.

"Well, Maddie if you're cool with it..." Shasta says.

"Cool with what?" Caleb says as he returns to the kitchen.

"Maddie's agreed to come shopping with us," Caroline says.

"Oh yeah?"

There's a spike in his voice, like he's not sure what's going on, but before it can be questioned by anyone (Caroline) he says, "awesome. You're gonna love Calistoga."

I finish what's left of my coffee and tell them I need just a few moments to get ready. As I'm coming out of the bathroom where the only thing that seemed fitting with my unruly hair was a high messy bun, Sarah barrels into me and wraps her arms around my waist.

"Why are you leaving? I don't want you to leave!" she wails into my legs.

"I'm just going out for a bit with your Aunt Caroline. I'll be back this afternoon, kiddo."

"I don't want you to go."

"I know, but you're gonna have fun with your mom, and like I said I'll be back this afternoon."

"Sarah, stop hanging on Maddie," Caroline hisses from the doorway. Sarah releases her grip and sticks out her tongue before running off down the hall. Caroline pulls a tube of lip-gloss from her purse and applies a thick coat as I sit on the shoe bench by the door and tie my chucks.

"Sarah's always super clingy," she says, smacking her newly glossed lips together. "It's annoying, right?"

I shake my head. "No, not really. She's a cute kid."

Caroline rolls her eyes. She rolls them a lot I've noticed. "They're all cute until they're not."

It's a good thing that Stephen's brother is so nice to Sarah and spoils her, because I'd wager, she probably doesn't get any attention from Caroline. In fact, Caroline probably pays more attention to her shiny lips than she does her own niece, and probably even her friends.

Caleb drives a lifted Rubicon. It's steel grey and he has to give me a boost just to get into the backseat. As we head into town, he drives a good twenty miles over the speed limit, but the windows are rolled down, the wind whips through the loose tendrils of my hair, and his base sounds amazing as a Macklemore song pumps through the speakers.

We find a spot at the far end of a parking lot and weave in and out of the various shops along the downtown, which is set up almost exactly like the Plaza in downtown Ashland. Even the shops are similar. More than a few wine stores, art galleries, gift shops, boutiques. Caleb loves antique stores, which I would never have guessed, mostly because I've never met a dude who liked to "antique." We spend a significant amount of time in a store called Roam Antiques which boasts "high end collectibles at a reasonable price." Spoiler alert, unless your "reasonable price" for say, a salt and pepper shaker set is $225 (on clearance!!!) well this is just not the store for you.

After Caleb does some damage there, we end our shopping at a cool vintage boutique called Mad Mod Shop which I actually liked for the plethora of 50's and 60's style fashion. I have zero fashion sense, but I've always admired people who can pull off the vintage look. And unlike most of the other stores, this one is reasonably priced.

By the time we stop for lunch I'm ravenous. Juicy, hamburger ravenous, so I'm thankful Caleb suggests we eat at a burger joint at the end of the block. After we give our orders to the server, Caroline digs her phone out of her purse while Caleb makes small talk with me.

"Alright, so," he takes a drink from his water glass, sets it down too rough, causing water to swish out. "You're from a Shakespeare loving town in Oregon, you just graduated high school, and you're spending the summer getting to know new family members."

"Yup."

"What's it been like? Finding out you have a half-sister and a grandmother? Is it wild? I bet it's just wild." His eyes bulge, like this whole scenario is the most interesting thing he's heard all week. Or ever.

"Um, I wouldn't say it's wild. More like surreal."

"Oh for sure," he says. "I mean, for Shasta, there was always a possibility of her having other siblings since she's always known she was adopted, but you didn't even know your mom had any other kids, right?"

I take a drink from my water and look around for the server, hoping to see her round the corner with our food so I don't have to partake in small talk any longer.

"Yeah that's right. No idea."

Caroline locks her phone and slides it back into her purse. "So why didn't she ever tell you?"

"About Shasta? I don't know."

"You must not have known her very well. I mean, what kind of mother keeps something like that from their own child? And for that matter, what kind of mother just abandons her child?"

"Hey, Caroline, I thought you were gonna ease up?" Caleb asks, sliding his hand across the table and brushing Caroline's fingers. It's a pretty intimate gesture, for them being just friends.

"What? We're just making small talk."

"Look, I've already said I don't know why my mom did what she did, or why she never told me about any of it. I'm sure she had her own, very personal reasons."

Before any more can be said, the server finally arrives with our food. We eat in silence. Caleb looks back and forth between me and Caroline, who just picks at the salad she's ordered, face turned up into a perma-scowl. I really am trying to give her the benefit of the doubt, but holy hell if she isn't a fucking bitch.

When we finish eating, I go to use the bathroom while Caleb offers to settle the bill. My hair is a big frizzy mess and my face and neck are splotchy thanks to Caroline and her rudeness. I splash water on my face and neck but it doesn't do any good. Just makes it look like I've tried to give myself a swirly. When I get back to the table there are three servers standing around having a heated discussion. When they see me, the one in the middle, who was our server points and then storms over with the other two.

"Were you seriously trying to dine and dash?" our server asks, hands on hips.

Say what now? "Uh I don't know what you're talking about."

"You were with the blonde guy with the surfer hair and the slender chick. I brought the bill to the table and when I came back to get it you were all gone. No money left at the table."

One of the three, wearing a manager tag clears his throat. "Miss, what you attempted to do is a crime, you do know that, don't you?"

By now all the restaurant patrons are staring at us. Didn't know they'd be getting lunch and a show. I'm beyond mortified.

"Okay there must be some misunderstanding. I went to use the restroom while my friend said he was going to pay the bill."

"Yeah well your friend kinda sucks because he just left and didn't pay," our server says. Her hands are still on her hips. The manager leans in and whispers something in her ear, she sucks in her lips and then turns to walk away followed by the other server. I'm left standing there with the manager and a dozen eyes from nosy patrons. My face feels like it's on fire, my throat is burning, and I my eyes are swelling with tears.

"I swear I had no idea they were planning to do that," I manage to choke out. "Please don't call the cops. I'll pay the bill."

Thankfully the manager is a stand-up guy, lets me pay the bill, and I'm out of there before I bawl in front of the entire restaurant. I walk to the opposite end of the boardwalk before I dive behind a building, keel over and sob. It's such a cliché move, like straight out of the 90's. *Hey, let's ditch the unwanted new girl with the bill and then leave her stranded in a town she doesn't know.* Thankfully I didn't have to scrub toilets, which is what they make you do in the movies, when they aren't arresting you. Thankfully I wasn't arrested! It's stupid moments like these, dealing with stupid mean girls like Caroline, when I really need Erin with me.

What am I even supposed to say when I get back to Shasta's and have to face Caroline? Caroline, with her stupid slender figure and that stupid bitchy smile. Ten to one she says she thought Caleb had paid the bill, and when asked why they left me behind…oh crap. How the hell am I supposed to get back to Shasta's? I could walk, but it's several miles and would take hours. City bus? Nope, no city bus here. Also, no Uber, not that I would even know how to get one since we walked everywhere in Ashland. I could hitch, but I'd probably get picked up by some sicko and wind up on an episode of *Unsolved Mysteries*. I do a quick search on my phone and find Calistoga has a cab company so I call one and get a ride back to Shasta's. I don't have her address, but wouldn't you know it, everyone knows Sweet Briar Cellars and the entire Green/ Callahan family. Halle-freaking-luiah!

It's well after five o'clock by the time I walk through the door.

"Hey Maddie!" Shasta calls from somewhere in the back of the house. "We're in the office."

I kick off my shoes, toss my bag on the bench and pad through the living-room and kitchen to find Shasta and Stephen at their computers. Through the large bay window, I can see Sarah playing on a swing set in the backyard.

"You were gone forever. Must have had a great time with Caroline and Caleb."

Okay, so I can do one of two things. I can tell her the truth, that her rotten little sister left me stranded with a restaurant bill and no way home, or be chill and make something up so as to not get Caroline into trouble. After all, maybe she was just pulling a prank and nothing more. Like a, *welcome to the family* sort of thing. Yeah right. No way in Hades she was just messing with me. She knew exactly what she was doing. I don't owe her anything.

"I take it you haven't seen or spoken with Caroline since we left?" I ask. Shasta looks at Stephen and then at me. "No. Is everything alright?"

"Yeah sure if you call dine and dashing while I was in the bathroom, leaving me to pay the bill and find my own way back to your place, alright-yeah everything is peachy."

"Wait, what?"

"Your sister's a real bitch, you know that?"

Shasta slinks down into her chair. Stephen runs a hand through his mop of hair.

"Wow," he says. "I mean, I knew she was having some issues with this whole new sister thing, but I didn't think she'd be that callous."

Shasta slides out of her chair and comes to stand in front of me. She opens her arms for a hug and after a moment hesitating, I walk into the hug. "I am so sorry she did that. She's twenty-two. A grown ass woman. She should know better. How did you get home? Please tell me you didn't hitch. There are psychos out there."

"I took a cab."

"Are you hungry?" she asks. "I was about to go make some dinner."

"Nah. I'm gonna go lie down if that's alright."

"Yeah no prob."

I slink upstairs to my room, falling into the soft plush of the comforter. It's early, but every part of me is exhausted and I want to forget about today.

June 15 1998

Hey Mama,

   The picture on this post card is of my actual studio. Can you believe it? I finally worked and saved enough to open my own place. It's amazing. I have the most amazing community. Also, I met a man. His name is William Crawley. He's British and a good guy.

   Namaste, Callie

Chapter Seven

TOMORROW is the Fourth of July. It's a big deal down here. The whole town gets involved. We're talking every house decorated in red, white, and blue banners, flags, painted rocks. There are bbq's, and fire crackers, even though I'm pretty sure that fire crackers are banned in the state of California. There's also a parade that runs down the main street, and people set out camping chairs and blankets the night before to secure their spots. I'm sure every town claims they have the biggest celebrations, my home town included, but the people here, well, it's a statement they swear by. This is what Stephen is explaining to me as he loads heaping piles of scrambled eggs onto the plate in front of me.

"And all the local vineyards and wineries walk in the parade giving out samples, like from a wine box," he says. "It's so crazy. You'd think there'd be some city ordinance on it or whatever, because it's alcohol, but there isn't. Well, I'm sure technically there is, but people just look the other way or something."

"That's bananas," I say, mouth full of eggs. "What do you guys normally do?"

Stephen grumbles as he sets the pan of eggs on the stove and slides into the chair next to Shasta. "Part of the deal with me getting the vineyard and my brother getting the winery is that we have to work together for the Fourth of July sampling."

"What does that entail?" I ask.

"Usually it means he sets up a booth downtown where the parade ends and we take a few shifts pouring samples."

"Do you guys ever get stuck working the booth at the same time?"

He lets out a laugh. "Thankfully, no. Kendall is really good with the schedule."

I gulp down the rest of my orange juice. "Hey, I want to help. Can I take a shift in the booth?"

"Oh, Maddie you don't have to do that," Shasta says, wiping maple syrup off Sarah's hands. "You're our guest. You should just come and enjoy the festivities."

"No really, I don't mind. I actually love working in booths. I used to work in the Wellsprings booths all the time back home. And during Shakespeare season I work the guest booths. Besides, I've spent so much time with Kendall in the office learning the business, I'm ready for a challenge."

"Well, if you think you're up for it," Stephen says.

"Totally. Just um, don't schedule me to work it with Caroline. For obvious reasons"

"Oh, you don't have to worry about that," Shasta says. "Caroline would never volunteer to work a booth."

The day after Caroline and Caleb ditched me at the restaurant, Shasta called her up and really laid into her. I mean it was gnarly. Like all the times I saw Maris and Erin fight but amplified to a thousand. Caroline swore up and down she didn't know where I'd gone after I said I was going to the bathroom. She claimed they waited and waited but when I didn't return, figured I'd decided to stay in town, because that sounds like something a person would do when they have never been to a town and have no possible way to get home. Oh, and assumed Caleb had paid the bill. Caleb will later say he thought Caroline had paid. After Shasta used some pretty colorful words, Caroline eventually owned up to what she'd done.

She even came over and had to apologize to me. It was a total bogus apology, too. Just words, no actual remorse. I accepted the apology because I'm clearly the bigger person, but that didn't mean I was in any way ready to hang out with her ever again. Thankfully she'd steered clear of Shasta's house the past two weeks, so I didn't have to pretend to get along.

When I told Erin about the great ditching, I was pretty sure she was going to tell her dad to fuck off and hop in her car and drive down here to rip Caroline's pretty head clean off her shoulders. I know we're best friends and all, and that means we tell each other everything, but sometimes I feel maybe it's best I don't tell her things like this, mean girl stuff, because she gets super angry super quick and I'm seriously afraid she's gonna snap. I just really hope there never comes a time when she does meet Caroline. It won't be pretty.

The morning of the Fourth, there's a note next to the fresh brewed coffee telling me that Stephen, Shasta, and Sarah had to leave to attend to a few things at the vineyard, but Caleb would arrive at 9am to take me to the booth. *Caleb? Why is Caleb coming to get me?* I wonder as I grab a travel mug from the cupboard, pour the hot coffee into the cup and add creamer. I pull my phone out of my back pocket and call Shasta, who picks up on the first ring.

"Hey, everything okay?" she asks.

"Yeah everything's fine, just had a few questions. A) what did you have to take care of at the vineyard so early and B) why is Caleb coming to get me?"

"Caleb works for us. Didn't I tell you? He drives the delivery van."

"Wait what? No, I didn't know that."

"Is that going to be a problem?" she asks.

"No, not really, I was just curious. You sure Caroline will be okay with him picking me up?"

"Why wouldn't she be?"

"Wouldn't it be like, crossing enemy lines or whatever? Him hanging out with me?"

"He's not going to be hanging out with you, he's just giving you a ride. It's not a big deal. Also, I'm pretty sure they aren't even dating anymore." Shasta makes some sort of garbled sound. "Hey Maddie? I really need to go finish loading the van. Can we talk all about this after the parade?"

"Yeah sure, uh see you la-."

She hangs up before I can even finish the sentence. I toast a bagel and sit out on the swinging bench on the porch to wait for my ride.

At nine sharp Caleb tears up the driveway, dust billowing up everywhere. The van is white, with the words "Sweet Briar Cellars" in curling rose gold paint. Caleb hops out of the drivers' side and walks up to the porch, leans on the rail.

"Hey there, Oregon. What's shaking?"

"Ack! Do not call me that."

"What? You don't like it?" he asks.

"That's a big Texas size 10-4 on that."

He tilts his head. "You say funny things."

"I've been told." I pop the rest of the bagel into my mouth, rinse it down with some coffee and hop off the porch, brushing past him on the way to the van.

We drive into town, abiding by all posted speed limits, which I can tell is really hard for Caleb to do because his foot keeps tapping on the gas and he hasn't stopped thumping on the steering wheel since we left.

"Hey so I should probably apologize to you, for the whole dine and dash thing," he says.

"Oh, you don't need to do that. Caroline already apologized."

He sucks in a puff of air, exhales. "Yeah but I shouldn't have gone along with it. It was a dick move."

"Really, it's okay."

There was no sense in being all pissed off at him. Caroline wouldn't have taken no for an answer. I don't know the dynamics of their friendship, did they date, are they dating, but he doesn't seem like the kind of guy who would do something like that without feeling bad.

He shrugs his shoulders, then thumbs around with the dial on the radio. "Let's find some music yeah? What are you in to?"

"I don't know. I don't really listen to a lot of music."

"What? You don't like music?" he asks.

"I didn't say I didn't *like* music, I said I don't listen to a lot of music. My mom used to listen to New Age and Americana stuff, my...step-dad...he listens to Latin music and my best friend likes hip hop so I'm always around music, but I just don't have a particular genre that I connect with."

He's looking at me like I've just recited the Magna Carta. "What? Why are you just staring at me?"

"I just have never met a teenager that wasn't obsessed with music, or at the very least didn't have a favorite kind to listen to."

"Yeah, well there's a first for everything."

"Ok, ok but gun to your head, what kind would you say you prefer to listen to?"

"Like if I had an actual gun to my actual head, and I had to decide right then right there? I guess I'd say...probably...indie folk rock, like The Head and The Heart. You've probably never heard of them."

He smiles, picks up his phone from the middle console, scrolls around and then while steering the wheel with his knees (*his actual knees!)* grabs the USB cord that's dangling from a port and plugs his phone in. He presses play and wouldn't you know it, an The Head and The Heart song sings out through the speakers.

"I love The Head and The Heart," he says and then sings along. He looks ridiculously cute, singing off key, hair flopping around like a shaggy puppy. I pinch a fleshy part of my thigh because I can feel myself starting to crush and this is just not what I want to happen.

"So, you're the delivery boy for my sister?" I ask.

"Yeah something like that. My dad and Stephen's dad are buds. When I was in high school my dad wrangled me into driving the van for the vineyards and then for the winery. I only have to do it on the weekends though so it's no biggie."

"What do you do with the rest of your time? Besides date the Devil of Napa?" I asked.

He smirks. "First of all, I go to school at UC Barbara. Pre-law. Second, Caroline and I aren't dating."

"You're not?"

"Nope. I mean, we used to date back in high school but she dumped me after graduation. Now it's just a casual thing."

"And they say romance is dead," I say.

"I like you kid, you're funny. So, what about you? Any boyfriends back in Oregon?" He pronounces it ORYGUN, and flicks a grin.

"Nope. No boyfriend."

"What about a girlfriend?"

I shake my head. "No girlfriend either. There was a guy I was dating for a bit, but my mom getting sick and then dying kinda put the relationship on the back-burner."

Oh no. He's now got that look on his face like he wants to say something deep and meaningful, like *sorry for your loss blah blah blah,* and I absolutely can't have that. Before he can say anything, I say, "Besides, who could possibly have time for boyfriends when they are getting to know a long-lost family?" He laughs and I'm all too aware at how much I'm staring at him. Straight white teeth. Smile that isn't crooked at all, blue eyes perfectly symmetrical. A laugh that is a carbon copy to Matthew McConaughey. Nope. I shake some pesky thoughts out of my brain right as we pull into the loading area of the festival where I see Shasta waving us over, a wiggly Sarah perched on her shoulders.

"Your destination, Madame," Caleb says and then winks. Before he can see me blush, I jump out of the van and speed-walk towards Shasta. Sarah runs over and crashes into me. She smells like cotton candy and her fingers are sticky. Again. Her fingers are always sticky.

"Maddie, Maddie guess what? I got to ride in a huge firetruck in the parade. It was awesome. I wasn't even afraid of the loud horn or anything."

"Oh wow that must have been fun."

"It was. I love firetrucks. Too bad it wasn't a monster truck. Grandma!" Sarah lets go of my leg and runs to Mrs. Callahan who is walking towards us with her husband. She scoops Sarah up and swings her around.

"Hello my little peach fuzz!"

"Grandma did you see me in the firetruck? I got to honk the horn!"

Mrs. Callahan laughs. "I did see you!"

She sets Sarah down and comes over to me, arms stretched out. "Hello Maddie, how are you?"

She pulls me in for a hug, and I sink in. I've only seen her three times since coming to Calistoga, but every time she hugs me, I feel comfort and acceptance, all the things you should feel in a hug. "I'm doing great, Mrs. Callahan, thanks for asking."

"Shasta tells me you're learning the business, eh?" she asks.

"Yeah I mean, figured while I'm here getting to know her, I should lend a hand. It's been pretty cool so far. I've learned so much about vineyards."

"Well, you'll love the carnival. All the wineries will have their samples, lots of good food and fun activities. I'm real glad you're here for this, honey."

She hugs me again and heads off with Mr. Callahan and Sarah. I finish helping Shasta and Caleb unload the van and then set up the booth with Kendall.

"Alright, looks like you're all set here," Shasta says, wiping her hands on her jeans. "I'm gonna go meet up with Sarah and my parents, but I'll swing by in about an hour to check on you. You sure you want to work the booth?"

I roll my eyes. "Shasta, I'll be fine! Go find your daughter."

"Girl she's got this," Kendall says, and does that finger snap thing. "She's learned from the best."

"Alright. Have fun," Shasta moonwalks off into the crowd.

Kendall straightens the glasses and wipes down the bottles of wine for the eighth time just as a gaggle of middle-aged women approach.

"Showtime," he says before flashing a smile, flipping back his hair and then addresses the group. "Hello how are you? Would you like to try some of our mouth-watering Pinot Noir, or our special Merlot?"

Two hours later, my feet are aching, I've got red wine stains on my shorts (I don't even know how that happened) and my face hurts from smiling so much. In my eighteen years of existence I don't think I've ever smiled that much. All in all though, it was an easy job. I poured the wine and offered the snacks while Kendall gave the spiel about the vineyard and how the wine is made at Vintage Cellars, yadda yadda yadda. By the time Paul arrives with our replacements and to check on the supplies, we've run out of samples and sold two cases of Merlot.

Paul scans the order sheets. "Wow Kendall, you've done it again."

"Was there ever any doubt?" he asks, jutting out a hip.

"Never in my mind." Paul turns to me and smiles. "You must be the famous Maddie I've heard so much about. My little niece can't stop talking about you." He offers his hand for a shake. "Hi. I'm Paul Green. Stephen's brother."

"Nice to meet you," I say, shaking his hand. He looks exactly like Stephen, which, why wouldn't he, they're twins, except Paul doesn't wear glasses and his hair is cut short, unlike Stephen's shaggy mane.

"How are you liking Napa Valley?" he asks.

"It's very nice. I mean, I'm sure I'd find it even more appealing if I were old enough to drink, but it's a beautiful area. Calistoga is awesome."

He cringes. "It's alright. I mean, I grew up here but now I live in Bloom. It's north of Calistoga, and a little less pretentious." He clicks his tongue on his teeth. "So. This must be weird for you huh? Meeting a family you never knew you had."

If I had a quarter for every time I've been asked this question. "Yup, pretty weird. But it's all good. I actually really like Shasta and Stephen, and the whole family. They're good people."

"Even Caroline?" he winks.

I hesitate. *Choose the right words, Crane. He could be setting you up.* "She has a plethora of fine qualities I'm sure she will show in due time." We both laugh. Kendall arches an eyebrow at us. He's probably questioning my loyalty. Shasta walks up with Sarah before anything else can be said. I see Stephen lingering off in the distance with the Callahan's. He looks at us and just as quickly looks away. Shasta cracks a smile as Sarah runs towards Paul.

"Uncle Paul! Uncle Paul!" she says, jumping into his arms.

"Hey squirt! I saw you riding in the firetruck! How fun was that?"

"It was it was SO fun. When I grow up, I'm going to drive a firetruck."

"I thought you wanted to be a monster truck driver?"

"I can do both Uncle Paul. Mom says girls can do anything they want."

Paul kisses the top of Sarah's head and sets her back down on the ground. "That they can little beans, that they can."

Sarah gives me a high-five before running to her dad.

"Hey Paul, how's it going?" Shasta asks.

Paul gives her a side hug. "I got no complaints. Business is good as ever."

She smiles. "Ah well, you're welcome. I worked really hard on the vineyard last year."

"Yeah but we all know I'm the one who actually runs the show," Kendall says from behind.

Shasta rolls her eyes. "Yes, Kendall we all know the vines would wither if it weren't for you."

He smiles and heads off into the crowd. "See you at work!" he yells as he goes.

"I'd better get the boys situated for their shift. Looks like a second wave is getting ready to come through. Maddie, it was a pleasure to meet you. I'm glad you got experience working the booth. Check out the rest of the carnival. It's great."

"Thanks, Paul. Good to meet you too."

We catch up to Stephen and Sarah who are busy sampling cheese and crackers. The grumbling in my stomach reminds me I haven't eaten anything since breakfast so I snatch up a handful of samplings.

"How was Paul?" Stephen asks Shasta. She shrugs, pops a hunk of cheese into her mouth.

"The usual. He just made some small talk and that was it."

"Did he ask about me?" he asks.

"Does he ever?" she answers. "Since when did you care if he asked about you? Thought you were totally fine never speaking to your brother unless actually forced to?"

"I *don't* care. I was just curious."

"Dad, I'm tired." Sarah tugs on Stephen's pants and then sits down at his feet. He bends down and lifts her up. She wraps her arms around his neck and leans in.

"I should get her home," Stephen says. "Are you guys okay hitching a ride with your parents?"

"Yeah no problem." Shasta smooths Sarah's hair out of her face and kisses her gently on the forehead.

"Is she okay?" I say as we walk around to find her parents.

"She just gets tired when she goes all day, especially if she doesn't sleep well at night."

I want to say, *well don't we all?* but I don't. "Does she often not sleep well at night?" I ask instead.

Shasta shrugs. "It really depends. She has Moderate Persistent Asthma, so sometimes she wakes up in the middle of the night having an attack. When that happens it's difficult to get her to go back to sleep."

"Is there anything that can be done for her? I mean, besides an inhaler?"

"She gets breathing treatments monthly and uses an inhaler a few times a day, but otherwise we just have to keep a close eye on her. Especially during high pollen count days. Anyway, c'mon. Let me show you around the carnival. The food booths are my favorite part."

We spend the rest of the afternoon with Shasta's parents, meandering the booths, sampling everything there is to sample, and of course being introduced to a million people because the Callahan's know everyone. By the time we get back to Shasta's, my legs feel like limp noodles from all the standing and walking. I call it an early night and crawl up the stairs, passing out the second my head hits the pillow.

June 15 2000

Mama,

I'm pregnant. You'll say this isn't the kind of news to reveal in a postcard, but when have I ever done anything in a proper way? I'm pregnant, and I'm going to keep the baby. I know you will probably worry, especially after the birth, but don't. William is a good man, a reliable man and will be a great father. I'm ready this time Mama, please believe in me.

Namaste, Callie

Chapter Eight

I KNEW I wouldn't be able to avoid the wrath of Caroline forever. I mean, who was I kidding, thinking I'd go the rest of my visit, however long it was going to be (I still haven't decided) never seeing Caroline again. But guess what? Calistoga really isn't that big of a town and so of course the odds I'd run into her somewhere, like say, a grocery store when I offer to go shopping for Shasta were pretty freaking high.

Shasta had to take Sarah to a birthday party, and Stephen had to work late in the office, so I offered to do the grocery shopping and make dinner for everyone. I'm no gourmet chef or anything but I've been known to whip up a mean pot of spaghetti. So that was my plan. Make spaghetti. There's a Starbucks in the same complex as the grocery store, so I pop in for a mocha before shopping. I'm standing in line for maybe all of two seconds, when up ahead I hear that familiar hair-raising laugh. I peer around the person in front of me and sure-freaking-enough there's Caroline at the front of the line with three of her lemmings placing their orders. I sweep my hair across my shoulder and try to bury my face, but she spots me. Her eyes narrow and her mouth turns up into this sinister-like grin before she wiggles her fingers at me. Then she's walking over to me with her lemmings in tow before I even have a second to try and push my way out the door.

"Well if it isn't my sister's other sister."

"Hello Caroline. How've ya been?"

"Just fine." She flicks her thumb back at her friends. "These are my girlfriends, Claire, Abby, and Eliza. Girls, this is Shasta's other sister, Maddie."

I do one of those semi-circle arm-waves and smile. The three of them stare, taking me in, probably trying to decide if any of the garbage I'm sure Caroline has spewed about me could possibly be true. The tall one with the nose ring, Claire, she's regarding me with the same look of distain I first got from Caroline, so I'm guessing she'll be the one who says something snarky to me. The one in the middle, Abby, she looks like she's not sure she should say hello back or what, but it's really coming across like she's holding in a fart. The third, Eliza, she's about my height with smooth chocolate-colored skin and long braided hair tied up into a low bun. She hits me with this ridiculously beautiful (and kind!) smile, and actually shakes my hand.

"Hi Maddie. Caroline's told us all about you."

"Uh-Oh. Well, don't believe everything she says."

Eliza smiles. "Don't worry, she didn't say anything bad."

Claire kicks at the floor with the tip of her shoe. "Just that your mom abandoned Shasta when she was like, a baby, and then took off for some hippie commune."

"There's a little more to the story," I say by way of a defense.

"But is it still true that your mom basically dumped Shasta in a dumpster right after she was born, and then she was found by some homeless dude?" Claire says.

I look at Caroline, beyond incredulously and say, "What? No. Caroline is that really what you told your friends? You know that isn't true."

Caroline just smirks and shrugs her shoulders. A freaking dumpster baby? I want to hurl something so hard at this callous bitch right now.

"No, my mom did not dump Shasta in some dumpster. She worked with an adoption agency *before* giving birth to find a family. It was a one-hundred percent legit, legal adoption."

"See, I told you Caroline was making it up," Eliza says. "For the record Maddie, I didn't believe it. I've known Shasta since I was nine and never did she say she was a dumpster baby."

"So like, why'd your mom keep it all a secret then?" Abby says. "She really must not have loved you very much to not be honest."

I'm just about ready to respond, either with words or fists, when the barista calls their names.

"That's us girls," Caroline says. "See ya around Maddie."

The lemmings turn without saying anything else, grab their drinks and leave. Eliza turns around at the door and mouths the words "I'm sorry" before leaving and now it's my turn to order but I'm so worked up and fighting back tears, I know I won't be able to keep it together long enough to order, so instead I run to the bathroom and lock myself inside where I cry, and it's the ugly kind of crying too.

I can't believe Caroline told her friends my mom hurled Shasta in a dumpster. Every part of me is shaking. It takes a special kind of rotten for someone to make up something like that. And for what? Because they're mad they have to share their sister with someone new? I don't even know if I should tell Shasta about today's encounter. Would she want to know what her sister is saying about her? I know Caroline's three friends are probably the most insignificant people ever, and so them thinking Shasta is a dumpster baby isn't going to mean much to her, but Shasta was super pissed, like *really* super pissed when she found out Caroline ditched me at the restaurant. She'd probably murder Caroline if she found out about the web of lies she's been weaving. I decide it's best to keep today's little interaction to myself.

***

I'm exhausted. Who knew spending an entire day in a van making deliveries throughout Napa Valley could take so much out of someone? I sure as hell didn't. I have new found respect for package delivery drivers, that's for damned sure. As tired as I am though, I actually had fun, which was not my intention at all. I thought assisting Caleb with deliveries would be mundane, maybe small talk here and there, but he made jokes, and created playlists, and we talked the entire time. He made it fun, and that's problematic, because I know if I continue to have these fun experiences with Caleb, I'm going to start crushing, and that little crush bubble will get bigger and bigger until it bursts into full on infatuation.

He swears up and down he's not dating Caroline, but I still feel like I'm crossing some line by even *talking* with him, which probably sounds ridiculous except for the fact that Caroline is one of the most terrifying women I've ever met. All she has to do is look my way and I feel my insides quaking, and not at all in the way they quake when Caleb looks at me.

I'm still thinking about how much I might be crushing when I walk inside Shasta's house at the end of a shift to find it completely empty. All the lights are still on, but I don't hear their voices, or television, or Sarah's laughter. Maybe they took a walk or something and just forgot to turn off the lights.

I set my bag down on the bench, slip off my shoes and pad through the living room to the kitchen in search of something to eat, then basically have a heart attack when I see Kendall bent over in the refrigerator. He must have been equally surprised because when he turns and spots me, he lets out a screech, slams the door closed and clutches his chest.

"Sweet baby Jesus!" He slides into a chair at the kitchen table. I scan the rest of the kitchen for any sign of my sister or Sarah but find nothing.

"Where is everyone?" I ask.

Kendall pulls his face into a sallow expression. "Uh well, they had to take Sarah to the emergency room."

"What do you mean they had to take Sarah to the emergency room? Is she alright? What happened?"

"Slow your roll, baby cakes. Why don't you sit down and I will make some tea," he says, and then pushes away from the table.

"No, I don't want tea, Kendall. I want you to tell me what's wrong with Sarah."

He sighs and slides back into the chair. "She had another asthma attack today while she was running around with the dog. The inhaler wouldn't work so they took her in."

"Oh no, is she going to be okay? Have you heard anything? Also why didn't anyone call me?"

"I haven't heard anything yet, and they didn't call because I was here when it happened and I said I'd stay and be here when you got back, so they could focus on Sarah."

It's kind that Kendall offered to wait here for me, but how hard would it have been to send a little text? Even just an emoji? I'm being stupid and selfish. Of course, she should focus on Sarah. I send her a quick text to let her know I'm thinking good thoughts for Sarah and tell Kendall to go ahead with the tea.. He's still clutching at his chest, and seconds away from bursting into tears, so it's the least I can do.

"I'd love some chamomile tea," I say.

He beams. "Coming right up."

While he fusses about making the tea, I heat up some left-over enchiladas and we sit in the living room with our food watching cooking shows on Food Network. Shasta brushed it off as being something not super serious, but if they have to take Sarah to the emergency room, I'm guessing her asthma is a bigger deal than she lets on.

I dig my tablet out of my bag and do an internet search on childhood asthma and find, yup, it can be pretty serious, like if you're sick, or around certain pollutants. Because I'm *ME* and think everything causes cancer, I check to see if she maybe has cancer instead of asthma, because you know, my assumptions and internet symptom check are better than an actual doctor. Nope, it's not cancer, it's just asthma. Still, my heart breaks for her because since the day I met her she's talked nonstop about her dreams of becoming a monster truck driver when she grows up. I doubt she'd be able to do that with her wimpy lungs and the crazy exhaust from the trucks.

I try to wait up, but I guess that didn't work out because one second, I'm watching *Pioneer Woman* and the next, the television is off and I hear clicking, like the sound of a key in the doorknob followed by the front door opening. I peer over the arm of the couch to see Shasta and Stephen shuffling in, a sleeping Sarah curled into her dad. There's a blanket on me, and my dinner plates are nowhere to be seen. I dig my phone out of my pocket and check the time. 2:30am. Shasta sets her purse on the bench and offers me a weak smile while gently removing Sarah's shoes. Stephen nods to me as he passes on his way up the stairs.

"Hey," I whisper, sitting up and tossing the blanket to the side of the couch. Shasta collapses next to me and lets out a deep sigh, kicks off her chucks.

"Hey," she says, eyes closed.

I lay the blanket over her and tuck it around her. "Looks like you could use this more than me."

She smiles, eyes still closed and pats my knee. "This has been the longest night ever."

"So is she gonna be okay?" I ask.

"Yeah. It's my fault really. She was playing outside with the dog and the pollen was really bad today, plus she'd already been coughing so much in the morning. I should have had her play inside."

"Is she going to grow out of this? I mean, can you even grow out of asthma?"

"You can, but her doctors aren't sure she will. She got really sick when she was a baby with RSV and ever since then she's always had trouble breathing. It's usually not so bad, but today was scary."

"How often does she need to go to the ER?"

"Twice, maybe three times counting tonight." She rubs her face with her hands, groans. "I am so freaking exhausted. I don't even think I can make it up the stairs."

"So don't. Sleep here. This couch is super comfy."

As I get up to go to my room she catches my hand. "Hey Mads, I'm sorry I didn't text you to let you know where we were."

"Don't even worry about it. Kendall was great. He made tea, we ate left overs, watched some tv. He even cleaned up."

She gives me a thumbs up before sinking further down into the couch. She'll be out in seconds. I'm not lying when I say that couch is comfy.

At breakfast Stephen and Shasta sport matching puffy eyes and move around the kitchen on auto-pilot. Sarah, who is usually zooming around the house by this point, is nowhere to be seen. I didn't hear any coughing fits, or panicked voices, so I'm assuming she slept through the night. Shasta and Stephen both look like they could use a year's worth of sleep. Maybe I can convince them to not go into work today.

I clear my throat. "What's say you guys play hooky and stay in bed? I'll hang with Sarah today."

Stephen groans. "Can't. Today's my day to help with the vines."

I turn to Shasta whose face is inches away from falling onto her toast. "Shasta? Wakey wakey. Can you stay home today?"

"Orders to fill," she mumbles. "Too many for Kendall to do by himself."

I laugh. "Ok A-you've met Kendall. Never tell him there's something he can't do and B-I can do it for you."

"I'll be fine. I just need a thousand more cups of this and I'll be good to go."

"Kay, but you're holding up a jar of creamer so I say no. Really, you guys. At the very least go in late. I can hang with Sarah for the day. Sleep and then go to work"

They look at each other and then back at me. "You sure?" Shasta asks.

I chug the rest of my coffee. "Positive. I'll throw some food on a tray and take it up to her, see if she's awake. If she's not, I'll just hang out and read a book until she does wake up."

"You're a freaking saint," Stephen says. He sets his mug in the sink and drags himself to the stairs, grazing the top of my head with a kiss on his way out. Shasta slides out of the chair and I watch as she zombie-walks to the living room, face-plants on the couch and buries herself under the blanket before I head upstairs with the tray of food.

When I get to her room, I nudge the door open and slip in, setting the tray down on her dresser. She's got her back to me, so I think she's asleep but the second I turn to leave, she rolls over and calls my name.

"Maddie, I'm hungry," she croaks. "And thirsty."

"Well, aren't you in luck, because I just so happen to have a yummy blueberry muffin and some ice-cold milk." I grab the muffin and the cup of milk, slide down to the floor next to her bed and wait for her to sit up before handing her the milk. She drinks half before asking for the muffin, which she somehow manages to eat in three bites. Erin would be impressed because we're talking Costco size blueberry muffins and this five-year-old woofed it down.

"Easy there, you're gonna choke." I hand her the milk and she chugs the rest.

"Nah, I got this. Can I have the banana?"

"As long as you don't try to shove the whole thing down your gullet."

She laughs. "What's a gullet?"

"It's your mouth. Or throat. I'm not sure which, let's just go with throat."

"Gullet. I like that word. Gullet, gullet, gullet." I peel the banana and hand it to her, thankful when she takes normal-sized bites. I set the peel on the tray and move the tray to the floor, then pull myself up to sit next to her on the bed with my legs stretched out across her Minions bed spread.

"So, I hear you're not feeling so great."

"Yeah I had to go see Doctor Vu last night. She works at the hospital. Have you ever been to a hospital, Maddie?"

"Uh yeah. I have, unfortunately. Several times."

"For being sick?" she asks.

"No, for someone else being sick."

She doesn't ask who. She takes a last bite of her banana. "I like Doctor Vu," she garbles. "She always has stickers."

"How are you feeling right now?" I ask. She shrugs her shoulders up and down several times.

"I'm probably like, eighty-five-point two percent okay."

I laugh. "Wow, eighty-five point two eh? That's oddly specific."

"Yeah. But I need to be feeling one hundred percent before Mommy lets me play outside. I don't like when I can't go outside. Did you know having outside time is g-r-e-a-t for you?"

"I did know that."

"Well, being stuck in here is not fun. I wish I could go outside."

"I know. I'm sure tomorrow you'll be better and can go outside. Today you need rest and I'm gonna hang out with you, so how about you pick out your favorite books and we'll read them and then play with your monster trucks together. Sound like a plan?"

We spend the morning reading every single book on her shelf, because apparently all of her books are her favorite, and then play with her trucks until she's yawning so much she can't stay awake. As she nestles down into her blankets and I tuck her in, she places her hand on my face.

"Can you lay with me for just a teensy second?"

"Sure, kiddo."

I lay down beside her and stroke her hair until she softly snores. I don't know how many times one of Leonard's sisters had asked me to chill with them and I said hard pass. It just wasn't my thing to chill with the littles. I don't know what it is about *this* particular little person. As I lay here, listening to her snores, little hands still smelling like bananas, I can't think of anything in the world I'd rather be doing.

January 9 2003

Dear Mamma,

I'm writing to let you know you were right, so go ahead and gloat. William left. He says it's only temporary, that he loves me and adores Maddie, but his desire for the theater is too strong to ignore. He was offered a role in a touring Shakespeare production, so he'll be gone for a few months. I still believe he is and will be an amazing father, but I guess he just can't be that right now. I'm going to try and respect that. Don't worry about us. We will be fine just the two of us.

Namaste, Callie

Chapter Nine

CAN someone be equal parts nervous *and* excited? I feel like I want to dance and throw up and I don't know which emotion is stronger. It's probably about 50/50. A little context-yesterday Rafe calls to say he's going to be doing an art exhibit in Sonoma and he wants to invite not just me and Shasta, but Shasta's WHOLE.ENTIRE. FAMILY, which includes her jerk of a sister.

"Are you sure you want to meet *all* of them? Wouldn't it just be easier to meet Shasta and Adelpha?"

"Nope, I'd like to meet them all."

"You're not just inviting them to fill the gallery with bodies, are you? Because your work speaks for itself and draws in a huge crowd of actual art lovers. You don't need to invite random people."

He chuckles. "*Mija*, they aren't random people. They are the people who raised your sister. I feel like it would be important to Callie for me to meet them, so just invite them. I'll have tickets for you all waiting at the door."

I thought for sure Mr. and Mrs. Callahan would have said no. They don't know this guy. He's not related to Shasta. He's not even technically related to me, but they were game. Apparently, they are fans of post-modern quasi-gothic art. Adelpha on the other hand, took a little more convincing.

"Sweetheart, the last time, and the only time for that matter, I saw this Rafe character, it hadn't been on so great of terms. There was a lot of yelling, mostly from me, and he just didn't see the best side of me."

"Well, that's all the more reason to come. He's not the type to hold grudges. He wouldn't have invited you if he was, and anyway I bet he doesn't even remember. That was so long ago, Adelpha. Please, it would mean a lot to me if you came. Rafe is a very important person to me, probably more than my own father."

After sighing and saying a bunch of things in Greek, she agreed and arrived early this morning. Okay, but why am I so nervous, you ask? Oh, I don't know, perhaps it's the fact that there's still this whole mystery surrounding my mom and her having given Shasta up, and I'm sure someone is going to bring it up, thinking Rafe will have the answers. Adelpha made it sound like she was embarrassed to face Rafe, but given what I know about her relationship with my mom when Mom was younger, what if she's actually the one with the issues? Or, what if Rafe meets them all and he doesn't like them? What if he says the wrong thing and it sets Caroline off? Hell, he could sneeze wrong and she'd pounce. I'm kind of hoping she'll decline the invite, if I'm being honest. After the coffee shop, I don't think I can handle another encounter with the she-beast.

Aside from all those stupid reasons to make me nervous, I really *am* excited to see Rafe. It's been two months since I came to California, the longest I've ever been away from home, away from Rafe, and I didn't realize how much I was going to miss him. I know I never told him enough, because what moody teenager wants to be real with their mother's long-term partner-boyfriend-whatever, but he's been there for all the real firsts in my life, and he loved my mother more than anything else, of that I was certain.

After Adelpha had arrived and settled in, she tells me she wants to go out for breakfast, just the two of us. We climb into her Volvo and head into town, stopping at a quaint restaurant called The Sassy Onion. It's easily become one of my favorite places to get breakfast, not just here but anywhere. I don't know how they do it, but their cinnamon rolls are the size of two of my faces and are pillow-soft. Not even the teensiest hard part around the outside that sometimes happens with cinnamon rolls. Oh, and their coffee tastes amazing, never burnt. Adelpha even finds their freshly made lavender tea satisfactory.

"It's not quite as good as the tea in my neighborhood," she says as she steeps the tea bag, "but it's hot and it's aromatic, so I guess it will do."

I dump four packets of Sugar in the Raw into my cup, splash in some cream.

"I know I said it a million times, Adelpha, but I'm really glad you drove up to meet Rafe. Well, meet him again."

She smiles and sips her tea. In the short amount of time I've known her, I've learned that when you say something and her response is a tea-sip instead of actual words, she really *really* doesn't want to talk about it.

"So, you've been here for several weeks. How has your visit with Shasta been?"

"It's actually been pretty great. I know I've been up here longer than intended, but..."

Adelpha waves her hand to cut me off. "Please, Maddie, don't apologize. You came to meet and spend time with your sister just as much as you did your grandmother. It's only right that you spend as much time as you need up here. I'm not going anywhere. Tell me, have things gotten any better with the other sister, Caroline?"

I roll my eyes and groan. "She's just the worst, Adelpha."

"Come now, I'm sure she's not that bad."

"Oh but she really is," I say, and then tell her about both the restaurant-ditching and the coffee shop encounter. "I don't even get it. Is she jealous or something? I mean, I've told her a million times I'm not going to be replacing her or whatever but she still insists on being a bitch."

Adelpha laughs and then covers her mouth with her hand.

"What?" I ask.

"Nothing, it's just you look just like your mother when you curse."

I smile and feel all the warms and fuzzies inside because I don't hear enough that I look like my mom. It's nice. I know that eventually, as Shasta starts to meet the people who were in Mom's life, if that's what happens next, she'll hear it all the time, how much she looks like Callie, and I will hear it less if at all, so I'm going to ride the wave as long as possible, even if the compliment only comes after I've cursed.

"Aside from the other sister, how has your time been with Shasta's family?

"It's been going great, I think anyway. Shasta's shown me the business and taught me some things, and we have late night tv sesh's, and it's been fun riding bikes together."

"Oh, Maddie that's wonderful to hear," Adelpha says.

"Yeah. I didn't expect to bond with her so quickly. I know in the beginning I was super hesitant, and kinda didn't believe any of it, but she's been chill and her family, for the most part, are cool too. Sarah, man she's just a real neat little kid."

"I do adore her. Such a precious spirit," Adelpha says.

"I'm not a little kid person, by any means, but she's just so cool. She's into rocks, and monster trucks, and she says things I didn't think a five-year-old would say."

"She's filled with a lot of spunk, that's for sure. I wish your mother could have met her."

"Yeah. Me too. She'd get a kick out of her, although it's weird to think of my mom as a grandmother," I say and Adelpha laughs.

"What's so wrong with being a grandmother?"

"Nothing, it's just Mom was always just my mom. I know she was in her fifties or whatever, and that's not so unusual, but Mom was just so youthful. It's hard for me to picture her as someone that someone *else* would call Grandma."

It's funny. The whole time my mom was sick, and then at her funeral, and even in the weeks after, I didn't like to talk about her with anyone. Not even with Rafe. I know it's a normal part of remembering someone and honoring them by talking about them, because talking regularly about someone keeps their memory alive, but I hated to do it. A knot would form in the pit of my stomach and get bigger and bigger until I felt I wanted to rip it out and then I'd be angry because the truth is, talking about my mom makes me angry. Angry that she got sick and that she couldn't be fixed. But everyone here wants to talk about her because they didn't get to know her. Shasta especially wants to talk about her, and while I've been able to tell her things about Mom, I'm never totally comfortable doing it. But talking with Adelpha about her, just now for example, I don't feel like I want to change the subject. I actually feel I want to talk more about her.

"I wish you'd been able to know her, my mom, you know, as I knew her."

"Me too, child. Me too."

***

Rafe is waiting for us outside the gallery. It's only 5:30pm and the exhibit doesn't actually start until 6pm, but I wanted to get there before the rest of Shasta's family does. I tell Shasta it's so that I can prepare Rafe for the family, but really, it's to prepare myself. Again, this is all so stupid, me feeling anxious, because Shasta's family (minus a certain bitchy younger sister) are great people. Rafe will like them (I don't think he's ever met a person he didn't like) and they will like Rafe. Everyone likes Rafe. What's not to like about him? He's tall, dark, and handsome, he's got just the faintest hint of an accent, and he can make a mean pot of Paella.

He greets us with a beaming smile and scoops me into his arms, kissing the top of my head. "Missed you, kiddo," he says. Then he turns to Adelpha.

"Mrs. Costas, it's been awhile," he says.

Her face is set into a straight line and I worry she's going to cuss him out, but then, the muscles of her face relax, and it's as if the years of harbored feelings begin to shed. Her lips curl into a sincere smile and she holds Rafe's hands in her own.

"Indeed, it has," she says. "It's good to see you, Rafe. I want to thank you again for the beautiful service you put together for my daughter. I'm sorry we weren't able to speak to one another at afterwards."

"Please, I should be the one apologizing."

She shakes her head. "Nonsense. You stuck with my daughter all these years and through her dark days. You helped her to raise a wonderful young lady. That's the best I could have hoped for."

They hug and I am relieved. All that anxiety had built up for nothing. I mean, it *could* have gone differently. She could have slapped him, spewed some Greek insults and stormed off, but I'm glad she didn't. I don't even know what status my heart would be in if she'd done that.

"Come," Adelpha says. "Let me introduce you to her eldest daughter, Shasta Green."

He gets a good look at her and gasps, touching the tips of his fingers to his lips.

"Goodness. You look just like my Callie." He pulls her into a hug. "It's wonderful to meet you."

"It's good to meet you too," she says. "Maddie's told me so much about you and how important you are in her life. This is my husband Stephen,-" they shake hands- "and this is our daughter Sarah."

Sarah sticks out her tiny hand and Rafe grips it, giving it a firm but gentle shake.

"Nice to meet you Mr. Rafe. Are you Maddie's Daddy?"

"Oh, Sarah well actually..." I start to say but Rafe jumps in.

"I think of her as my daughter, yes. I've raised her since she was five."

"Hey! That's how old I am!" she exclaims. He laughs, deep and animated. It's the kind of laugh that makes you want to tell jokes over and over again just so you can hear it all day. "Maddie said you are a painter. Guess what? I paint too, and I painted you this picture." She pulls a folded-up piece of construction paper from the pocket of her sweater and hands it to him. He unfolds it, smiles, and then turns it over so we can all see it.

"Sarah, this is wonderful! Can you tell me about it?"

"Oh yeah. These right here," she points to a glob of purple dots, "are grapes because that's what my family does. We grow grapes. And this is the sun because you need the sun to grow the grapes, and this right here," she runs her fingers down a blue line, "is the river that is in our yard. Mommy says I can't go down there by myself, but sometimes my uncle Paul takes me."

"I think this is amazing. Do you know what? I'm going to include it in my exhibit. Would you like that? Would you like this to be on display?"

"Well, I don't know what "display" means, but I painted it for *you* so if you want to display it that's cool."

He laughs. "Alright. That's very cool."

Somewhere in the far corner of the parking lot we hear an engine backfire, so I know the Callahan's have arrived. Mr. Callahan drives a station wagon from the 70's that is somehow still running, but packs a mean backfire that I've been told scares the shit out of people in a school zone.

I'm crossing my fingers behind my back as I watch Mr. Callahan climb out of the car and then come around to the other side to open the door for Mrs. Callahan. I uncross them, maybe swear a little under my breath as I see him open the rear passenger side door and Caroline steps out, smoothing down her skirt and flicking her high pony tail like she's Ariana Grande. Would it have been so much for her to decline? Nah. She'd want to take any chance she got at once again talking shit about my mother.

"You sure you want to meet Caroline?" I whisper to Rafe. "Not too late to say it's a full house."

He nudges me with his elbow. "I'll be fine." He plasters on the biggest smile and walks right up to Mr. Callahan, hand extended.

"Mr. and Mrs. Callahan, it's a pleasure to meet you. I'm Rafe Giancarlo." After he shakes Mr. Callahan's hand, he scoops Mrs. Callahan's up in his, brings it to his lips and kisses it; her face turns beet red.

"Good Lord, I don't think I've ever had my hand kissed in a greeting before," she declares.

"What a travesty, a woman of such beauty as you are."

Classic Rafe. He's laying the debonair on super thick, and you'd think it was all for show, but believe it or not, that's one hundred percent authentic Rafe. My mom told me that when she first met him, he'd leave a red rose right outside the door to the yoga studio every day. After a month of doing this, she finally agreed to date him. And then once a month he'd give her a bouquet of thirty roses, one for every day it took to win her over. He's just a romantic, super suave dude. Know who isn't buying any of it? Yup. Caroline. He extends his hand to greet her and it stays there in the air, left hanging until Shasta kicks at her foot and she finally shakes his hand.

"Caroline, it's nice to meet you."

She looks at Shasta, catches the narrowing of her eyes and the smallest shake of her head, and says "Nice to meet you too."

I let out the deep breath I wasn't even aware I'd been holding in, and my shoulders relax. Saved by the older sister *don't-you-dare look*. I know she'll find a way to say something mean later, when Shasta isn't around. I know this because as we all walk in behind Rafe, Caroline brushes past me, knocking my shoulder with hers, and then shoots a nasty glare over her shoulder at me. I need to stay on guard tonight.

We're an hour into the exhibit. So far no verbal assaults or drive-by snide comments from Caroline. Actually, Shasta's had her on Sarah-duty while we mingle. She looks royally pissed about having to babysit instead of attempting to carry out a sabotage. I didn't tell Shasta about what Caroline told her friends, so I'm guessing Shasta is just being overly-cautious. I think she's started to realize just how capable her sister is at being a royal bitch and since she knows how important this meeting is for me, I have to give her some mad props for keeping the she-beast occupied. Of course, it hasn't stopped her from shooting daggers at me.

I stick close to Rafe as he takes us around and introduces us to the other artists, and then in the lag time before all the artists are expected to give a quick speech about their selected works of art, Rafe is asked all sorts of questions by the Callahan's-*at what age did he take an interest in painting, who would he say his biggest inspiration is, how long has he lives in Ashland, what part of Spain are his parents from*. They are the sort of questions that I'd find annoying. Yeah sure, if you want to get to know someone you have to ask all these stupid questions, but sometimes I just think the way to get to know a person is organically, letting things come up as they do rather than asking questions like you're reading down a list. Rafe doesn't seem to mind though. He seems to be enjoying himself.

After the speeches, I'm walking around checking out all the collections and I spot Rafe and Adelpha sitting at a table by the bar, and at first, I'm thinking they are arguing because of the way her face is twisted up, and she's dabbing at her eyes with a napkin, but then she smiles and touches Rafe's face. He places his hand on hers and then he gently pulls her into a hug. It makes my heart happy, but also sad because while I'm glad Rafe and Adelpha were able to bury the hatchet, I wish Mom and Adelpha had been able to as well. I wish I understood more about the nature of their relationship and why it had always been so challenging.

I'm thinking about my mom and how much I miss her, when I see Mrs. Callahan standing in front of one particular painting of Rafe's, that for obvious reasons is my absolute favorite. My mother, painted a few months after we learned she'd stopped responding to treatment. Mom went to stay at the Wellsprings for a few days, and Rafe holed himself up in his studio. I don't think he even came out for coffee. Three days later he emerged, totally disheveled, set the painting in the living room and left to pick up Mom.

It's a 30 inch by 72 inch canvas acrylic painting of my mother sitting on a park bench. Half of her is dressed in a deep purple floral dress that knots around the neck, while the other half is in a tattered pale blue hospital gown. The left half of her hair is billowing around her in chestnut curls, adorned in yellow and purple zinnias, her favorite flower, while the other half of her hair is thin and stringy. She's smiling, but it's the kind of smile you can fake when you feel dead inside, and her eyes are looking up into the sky and her left hand is outstretched, and there's a pair of cracked misshapen hearts in her palm. It's a swirl of colors and jagged edges. Mrs. Callahan stares at it and a single tear rolls down her cheek as I come to stand beside her.

"It's exquisite," she whispers.

"It's my mother," I say. "Rafe's a very emotional guy, and he has no problems articulating his feelings, but they always come out best in his paintings.

"It's just so raw, so real." She wraps an arm around my shoulders. "Honey, I am so sorry for what you've had to go through. Losing your mother at a young age."

"Thank you. I appreciate it."

She kisses the top of my head and walks away. I wipe my eyes and turn to find Caroline standing behind me.

"What was that about? You and my mother?" she hisses.

"It wasn't anything. We were looking at the painting and she felt like giving me a hug."

"You know, just because you lost your mother doesn't mean you can have mine."

And there it is. I knew she wouldn't be able to go a whole evening without saying something cruel. "I'm not trying to take...you know Caroline, this is really getting old. I don't have time to deal with your issues."

She's about to respond when Sarah pops up next to her dancing. "Auntie Caroline, Mommy told me to ask you to take me to the bathroom."

"I'll take you," I say, but Caroline glares and grabs Sarah's hand.

"I've got it," she hisses and stalks off with Sarah in tow towards the bathroom. I really don't like to think of myself as a violent person, I mean we all know that in my circle of friends Erin is the muscle and I'm not, but this freaking girl makes me want to slam her head into something hard.

Rafe has to leave around noon the following day, but we decide to squeeze in a brunch date before he goes. I borrow Shasta's car and meet him at a small restaurant that specializes in omelets. In the hierarchy of breakfast eggs, it goes from bottom to top, fried (over medium because sunny side up is gross) scrambled (but only with copious amounts of cheese) and omelets. Doesn't even matter what kind. Traditional Denver omelets, veggie omelets, just plain ole cheese omelets. I love omelets.

He's already there when I arrive, and I'm not surprised at all to find he's on his third cup of coffee.

"Aren't you worried your gut will rot with all that caffeine? I know you'll have more sometime this afternoon, and your usual glass of red wine at dinner."

"Nonsense. I have a strong gut. Besides, this isn't even strong coffee. Here, I ordered you a cup."

He slides a mug across the table and I drink. He's right, it's weak, but it's caffeine so I don't complain.

"Be honest. Did you like the family?" I ask.

"They are wonderful people. Mrs. Callahan is such an animated woman. She was a joy to be around. Her husband, is he always so quiet?"

I laugh. "Yeah. He's a nice dude, but he rarely says anything. Smiles a lot and I know he likes to laugh, but he's not too keen on the whole talking thing."

"I just can't get over how much Shasta looks like your mother."

I grumble.

"I thought you liked Shasta, *Mija*?"

"I do! I like her a lot it's just, that's the first thing I'm ever going to hear any time someone meets her, how much she looks like Mom and how much I...don't."

He slides a hand across the table and takes mine. "You may not share her looks, but you share her spirit. She loved you more than life itself and you'll always carry that with you."

"Thanks."

"But really, has it sunk in yet? That you have a sister? A niece?" he asks.

"I don't know. I guess I'm still trying to figure out what it all means. We get along great. We can talk for hours, but also, we can just sit in the same room, not saying anything all day and it's not weird. I think Sarah is the neatest little kid, I just wish that Caroline didn't hate me so much."

"I wouldn't take that too much to heart. She's just jealous."

"Yeah, tell me something I don't know, Rafe. I *get* she's jealous but I don't get why. I'm not replacing her. I don't know why she can't see it as gaining a sister or at the very least a new friend."

"Her mother explained that Caroline has always had a difficult time maintaining meaningful friendships. What was the expression used? She goes through friends like tissue paper. Aside from some boy, her sister has been her only constant her whole life."

I think of her three lemmings I met at the store and wonder what she's paying them to hang around her. "Well, that still doesn't give her a reason to be mean all the time. Did you talk to her at all? Beyond the initial meet and greet outside the gallery?"

He shakes his head. "No. I tried to engage but she shut me down."

"Still want me to feel sorry for her?"

"I'm not asking you to feel sorry for her, I'm just asking you to understand. Have grace," he says. Was that something I was even capable of having? Grace for someone like her? My entire life growing up, Mom prescribed to a more Buddhist way of life. She lit her incense, said her mantras, meditated and taught me that people deserved more credit than you think they should be given, second chances are always necessary, and treat everyone with respect. But what about if other people aren't treating you with respect? What if the other people are acting like heinous little bitches? She'd say that's probably when it's needed the most, but with Caroline, my brain tells me there are two ways to approach her. The Callie Crane way of respect and understanding even in the face of bitchiness, or the Erin Whitney way-take zero shit and put her in her place. Currently, I'm leaning towards the latter.

"Just try to enjoy what's left of your summer getting to know your sister. Speaking of end of the summer, have you decided what you're going to do in the fall?"

I have been putting off telling Rafe that I've officially asked for a deferral. I haven't even told Erin or Leonard. We were all supposed to head up there together. Erin sends a text almost every day reminding me of things to bring and making sure I select the right freshman dorms. I've been meaning to tell her, but I just don't want to piss her off.

"You're not going to school, at least not yet anyway," he says.

I look up at him in shock. "Why do you say that?"

"Honey, I know you. I can tell by the look in your eyes you're not ready to leave yet. That, and your request for a deferral was granted. They sent a letter and called the house. They want you to call them back to talk out the details." He smiles, takes a sip from his coffee. Not sure why they called the house phone instead of my cellular, but oh well. At least the cat's out of the bag.

"You're not mad?" I ask.

"Why would I be mad?"

"Because! Because I promised Mom that I would stick to the plan and go to college."

He finishes the bite of egg on his plate and wipes his face with a napkin. "Honey, you know just as well as I do that when it came to your mother, lines were not fluid. You could be called to do a handful of things in your life but none of those things have to go in order or according to a plan. You promised her you'd go to college, and I am sure she knew that it meant you'd go on your own time. If you feel you need to continue on with your break, if you're not ready, I fully support you."

I think in my heart of hearts I knew this, knew that when I made that promise to my mother, for her it wasn't so much that I actually continue on with my education. Seeking a four-year university degree was never anything she stressed upon me growing up. For her, if you had a plan for your future, even if that plan was going to change by the time you got there, that's what mattered. I also think she just didn't want me sticking around town wallowing. She wanted me to live my life. But the truth of the matter is, I really *don't* know what I want to do with my life. The only thing I do know is that I'm not ready to go to school, not just yet.

"Thanks Rafe, it means a lot."

"Any time *Mija*. Just make sure you call the school, and be honest with your friends. Well, I need to hit the road." He flags down the waitress to settle the bill.

"Where are you heading now? Back home?"

"Not quite. I've got two more galleries down in LA and then I'll head home."

We pay and then walk to our cars where we say our goodbyes. I watch him until he is down the road and out of sight, then climb into Shasta's car. I don't feel like going back to her house yet. Adelpha is only sticking around for a little while longer, and I'm sure she wants to spend more time with me, but I just need space to clear my head.

I start the car, kick the gear into drive and head to Mountainview Park. It's this small park on the top of a hill that has an awesome panoramic view of basically every vineyard in the valley. There's a small duck pond, a few benches dedicated to the founders of the town, and this really neat fountain made to resemble the Treve Fountain. It takes me awhile to find it on my own since the only other time I'd been here was with Shasta when she was driving me around the town, but I find it, or rather Siri finds it, and I park along the gravel road and make my way towards the fountain.

The mid-morning sky is a hazy blue, and it's warm even with the breeze. I love this weather. Back home, with it now being mid-August, every day would be blisteringly hot with zero breeze to offer any reprieve. Sure, there's the river and the lake but both are usually super over-crowded, and the jet boats always get in the way of really enjoying the river. I just now realize this is the first summer that Erin, Leonard and I won't be floating the river. It makes me sad, thinking about the changes, but I guess that's what life is supposed to be, right? A series of life-changes that invariably happen, and the importance of just going with the flow. That's probably the biggest thing I'm learning here meeting my family. You just have to go with the flow and take whatever crazy is handed out. I'm just glad that Shasta is such a chill person. I can't even imagine if she'd turned out to be this lame person I was stuck with as a sister. Would I even want a person like that as a sister? Holy shit, what if Shasta was exactly like Caroline? Would I be like "peace out, nice knowing you but no thanks to this whole sister thing"? I'm deep in thought staring into the fountain when I see a reflection take up space next to mine. For a half second, I freak until the other reflection cracks a smile, one I have come to know well, and I relax.

"Don't sneak up on girls," I say as I turn around. Caleb has his back to the sun, so I have to raise my hand to my forehead to shield my eyes in order to look at him. "You're like, in the perfect spot for a junk punch."

He laughs. "Are you saying you'd actually punch me in the balls?"

"I'm saying, if you sneak up behind a girl, especially one who has taken several self-defense classes, you run the risk of a junk punch. That's all. What are you doing here?"

"You're not the only one who enjoys the solitude of Mountainview Park." He holds up a bag containing hunks of bread. "I like to feed the ducks."

"That is such a strange thing to like to do," I say.

"Why is that? You think because I'm not a ten-year-old boy or a ninety-year-old man that I can't enjoy feeding hunks of day-old bread to ducks?"

"Yeah, pretty much. Doesn't seem like the type of interest Caroline would approve of."

He narrows his eyes at me and holds out a hand. "Want to join me?"

"Why the hell not." I grab his hand and we jump down and walk over to the edge of the pond. He offers me a hunk of crusty bread. We break off bits, toss them into the murky pond. A raft of grey-headed ducks swims as quick as they can to the soggy hunks of bread. I don't tell this to Caleb, but I actually like feeding ducks as well. I mean, how can you not when there's a duck pond, nay two, basically in front of your house. My mom used to teach sunrise yoga in Lithia in the summers and since yoga has never been my thing, I'd wait for her at the pond with my books or schoolwork and kill time feeding ducks. When she and Rafe were finished, they'd usually join me and we'd have a picnic.

I palm my hunks of bread and kneel down, stretching my hand out so the ducks can swim up and take them from my hand.

"You know there's probably like a hundred diseases in those things," Caleb says.

I laugh. "Just a hundred?"

"So real talk, how come you're not hanging out with your sister and grandma? Why are you traipsing around town alone?"

"Why are you?"

"I asked you first."

"I'm sure you know my...well I don't ever actually know how to refer to him. He's not technically my stepdad but saying my mother's partner doesn't sound right either. Screw it. My dad Rafe was in town last night for an art exhibit and he invited the family out to come."

"The whole family? Caroline included?"

"Yeah. She didn't tell you? Figured she would have."

"We actually haven't hung out in a while. Not since the whole restaurant ditching."

I look the other way to hide my smile. I don't know why this is good news to me. It's not like we're going to start dating now that I know he's really truly not with Caroline. I don't even think he likes me that way. Hell, I'm not even sure I like him that way. Ok lie. I like him that way.

"Did he like the Green's and the Callahan's?" Caleb asks, chucking his last hunk of bread out into the middle of the pond.

"Oh for sure. He thought they were great people."

"Totally not surprised. Everyone loves them."

"Was Caroline nice?" he asks.

I chuck a hunk of bread at him. "I think you know the answer to that."

"Fair point," he says.

"I was just glad that he and my grandma made amends." I start laughing and he gives me a funny look.

"Did I miss the joke?" he asks.

"No, it's just that this is the first time I've actually referred to Adelpha as my grandma."

"That's good, right? I mean, isn't that what your whole trip has been about? Getting to know a grandma and a sister?"

"Yeah but my whole life I've only had one woman I call Grandma, and I've never associated that word with a deep emotion, you know? But when I just said the word in regards to Adelpha, there was love. I don't think I'm explaining this very well."

He shakes his head and smiles. "No, I totally get it. I'm super tight with my grandparents on my dad's side, but my mom's parents live in Indiana and they're ancient. I've only seen them maybe a handful of times so it's not like a really know them."

"Yeah, and my grandparents are in England and I've only seen them in person four times!"

"Four?"

I nod. "Yup. They came to visit when I was a year old, but I don't count that since I can't remember it, and then they came again when I was seven, and when I was twelve, I went with my dad to visit them in England. Most of our interaction has just been texts and Zoom calls. Also, they aren't the big sentimental type, so keeping in touch and sending cards and all that isn't really their thing."

My phone buzzes in my pocket. I pull it out, see it's a text from Shasta.

"My sister. She needs me to bring the car back."

"Bummer. I kinda liked this little moment we were having, Ashlander," he says, and smiles his stupid beautiful smile.

I shake my head. "Nope, don't call me that either."

"Alright fine, I'll find something that sticks."

There's no way he's not seeing me full-on blushing right now. "Good luck with that."
I turn and head for the car fighting the urge to look back.

October 5 2005

Hey Mamma,

I hope you're well. Things are good with us, great even. I've met someone; we've been seeing each other for several weeks. Don't worry, he's nothing like William. He's an artist, but he's grounded, stable, and you should see the way he dotes on Maddie. I hope you'll come and meet him. I'm sorry for the way things have been the past few years. Please come visit.

Namaste, Callie

Chapter Ten

"I CAN'T believe you're ditching me." It's Erin. We're FaceTiming. I'm curled up on my bed and Erin is running around her room scooping up articles of clothing and shoving them into duffel bags. I'm not even sure if anything is clean because she's known for just dumping her clean clothes on her floor, sometimes right next to her dirty clothes, with the intentions of folding and putting away later. Yeah, this never happens. Everything stays exactly where it's dumped.

"You're going to be fine, Erin."

"Yeah but I had to apply for a new roommate! Do you know how much that sucked? What if she's like super goth or whatever like the first roommate Maris had?"

I finally contacted the University of Oregon about my deferral. They said at first, they'd been reluctant to grant it because I'd waited for so long to apply, and even longer to call them back, but given the nature of my circumstance and how sweet my "step father, who by the way, has the most amazing accent" was on the phone, they agreed to defer me a year. They call it a "gap year" or whatever. Rafe said he was going to stick by his statement that he was fine with it, so long as I *did* come back to town at some point. Erin on the other hand was super pissed. She didn't even talk to me for three days, which is the longest we've ever gone without talking to one another. It was lame. Then I guess Leonard talked some sense into her because she called and said she understood, but still hated the idea of going off to college without me.

"It's going to be fine, even if your roommate is goth."

"Well, she won't be because I'm rooming with Maris," Erin says. I gawk at her and she smiles.

"You're rooming with Maris? What's with all the theatrics then about having to get a new roommate?"

"Just wanted to give you a hard time. You know, for ditching me."

"I'm not ditching you, Erin. I just need more time."

"I know!" she whines. "I'm just going to miss you."

"I'll miss you too, but you'll have Leonard, and Maris."

Erin tosses the stuffed duffel bags onto the floor and stretches out on the bed on her stomach, resting her chin in the palm of her hands.

"So what *are* your plans anyway?" she asks. "You just gonna stay in Calistoga working at the vineyard?"

"Um, I don't know yet." The truth is, I've loved the time I've spent this summer getting to know Shasta and her family. I really feel like we're sisters, but ever since running into Caleb at the park, all I've wanted to do is hang out with him, and I shouldn't want that. I should be going back to spend more time with Adelpha.

"It's Caleb, isn't it," Erin says. Damn, she's good.

"What? No. It's not about him at all."

"You're such a bad liar Mads. Just admit it. You like him."

"Well even if I did it's not like we could date or whatever. His whole life is here, mine's in Oregon. Long distance would suck. Also, Caroline would never let it happen."

"She doesn't own him. Caleb is his own person; he can talk to and date whomever he wants."

"Yeah, you try telling that to Caroline."

"You want me to come and kick her ass? There's still time. I don't have to be at school for another day."

I laugh. "You're ridiculous."

"Will you at least promise to be home by Thanksgiving? I am going through some serious BF withdrawals and I cannot watch the parade and holiday lighting without you."

I grin. "Yeah, I'll make sure to be back by Thanksgiving."

I spend the rest of the afternoon chilling with Sarah, playing with her trucks and painting rocks. She hasn't had any of those wicked coughing fits in a few weeks. While we paint, I think about my options for the rest of my time here. Obviously, I want to stay here and spend more time with Shasta and Sarah, and okay, fine, with Caleb, but ever since the night of the art show, Caroline has been showing up more often at the house, and she's never nice, no matter how hard I try to be kind. If she shows up when Shasta and I are watching one of our trash shows, she'll wedge herself in-between us and bash the shows, and flick us shit for watching them. Worse though, when she and her parents come over, she blocks me from even talking to her mom.

Shasta won't admit it, but I know it's taking a toll on her. She tries her best to smooth things over, stop Caroline before she really gets started, but then they just fight with one another and I end up feeling like I'm getting in the way of two sisters. Yeah, technically I am Shasta's sister as well, but I mean, sometimes you can be blood related to someone but not think of them as family at all, and sometimes it's the opposite. I think of Rafe as my dad, and Roxy as my aunt because my mom considered them to be her family. It's clear that Caroline will never in any way think of me as part of *her* family, and I didn't know what that would end up meaning for me and Shasta. Would I just be this person she was related to that she saw occasionally? Like would she say "oh I have two sisters but one is just like a quasi-sister." Bleh. I just wish Caroline wasn't such a bitch about it. There's no good reason why we can't be friends, but I know you can't make someone like you.

Then there's Adelpha. There's still so much she hasn't told me about my mom. There has to be more to her story. I want to hear more about how Mom was as a baby, a kid, a teen. Did she love any other bands besides The Cure and The Smiths? Her room is littered with concert tickets, band posters, maps with places circled. Did she ever get to any of the circled places? There was this whole person before she gave birth to Shasta and upended her whole life. Shasta may have been content enough with her adopted parents to not be curious, but I need to know who that person was and more about why she and Adelpha didn't get along, because my mom and I never fought.

But maybe there isn't more to the story. Maybe Mom was tired of her rebellious lifestyle, not ready to be a parent, and left town to get a fresh start. There's no crime in that. I still don't get why she felt she couldn't tell me any of it, and in my heart of hearts I know I won't find the answers in any of her boxes of mementos, but maybe if I spent more time with Adelpha, it will be like she's getting some form of closure with my mom. However nutty that might sound.

As much as I'll miss being around Sarah and her spitfire ball of energy, and the late-night talks with Shasta while we watch reality tv, I need to go. After dinner I call Adelpha and talk to her about me coming back and she's beyond excited, so I tell her my plan is to stay here with Shasta until the end of the week and catch a bus to San Francisco.

"Nonsense," Adelpha says over the phone. "You're not paying for a bus. I will come get you."

"It's not that big of a deal, Grandma, Erin and I used to take the bus up to Portland all the time to visit her mom."

"I'm coming to get you."

I know already there's no point in arguing with her, so we plan on Saturday. Now I just have to tell Shasta, which I do after she and Stephen put Sarah to bed.

"Hey guys, can I talk to you for a second?"

"Sure, what's up?" Shasta flops down next to me on the couch.

"So, I've had a super great time staying with you guys, and you've been so kind to teach me your business but..."

"Wait," Shasta cuts me off. "Are you leaving?"

"Uh yeah. I think it's time for me to go back to Adelpha's."

"Was it something we said or did?" Stephen asks.

"No, it's nothing like that."

"Was it Caroline?" Shasta asks with a horrified look on her face. "Did she do something again? She told me she was going to back off."

"No no it wasn't anything Caroline did. I mean, she's been a royal pain in the ass, especially lately, but I promise you, this doesn't have anything to do with her."

"Ok, Maddie, I know I've only known you for a few months, but I can already tell you're a bad liar."

I smile. "Yeah, so I've been told." I pause before continuing. "I feel like Caroline is never going to let up, and I don't want to be the reason she like, disowns you or whatever. Plus, I really just need to spend more time with Adelpha before I go home in November."

Shasta's eyes well up. "I really don't want you to go."

"I know, but I mean, I wasn't going to stay here forever. I have a life in Ashland, I have things I need to sort out, and I still technically have to go to school at some point."

Shasta smiles, wipes her eyes. "I get it. We got so used to having you here, I forgot you don't actually live here."

"I've really appreciated you letting me spend so much time here. But I need to go."

"When do you want to leave?" Stephen asks.

"Adelpha said she'd come get me on Saturday."

Shasta shakes her head. "Stephen and I were thinking of having a party here on Saturday for my parent's anniversary. You have to be there for that."

"Yeah," Stephen says. "It just wouldn't feel right without you."

How can I say no to a party?

***

We have the party at the Callahan's. Shasta's house would have been fine but she said her parents have a backyard to die for, and she wasn't kidding. There's a massive deck spanning the length of the house with an outdoor kitchen and a brick pizza oven. The far end of the yard is lined with rows and rows of olive trees. To the left is a koi pond, and next to it is a fire pit surrounded by plush green lawn chairs. I help Shasta and her mom spend the better half of Saturday morning decking out the backyard, and when we finish, well, let's just say it's what I imagine a fairy wedding looks like. Strands of twinkling lights tucked into crème colored tulle are strung from the deck, and even more connecting to the rows of trees. Wooden picnic tables are covered in lavender and white colored tablecloths; mason jars filled with sprigs of lavender and artificial tea lights placed in the center of each table.

A massive buffet table up on the deck is filled with so many types of dishes I can't keep count, and Mr. Callahan has rolled out his signature drink, which is supposed to be similar to a sangria, but it smells like fruity gasoline.

It's just after 6pm, still early enough in September that there's plenty of daylight, but there's a crisp evening breeze that causes the lights to gently sway. It's absolutely stunning.

"Shasta, this place looks amazing," I say, as we slide serving spoons into dishes. "I don't really have an eye for any of this."

"Thanks. I learned from my mom. She used to be an event planner before she married my dad."

"My mom was horrible at decorating. She didn't like for anything to match so our living room is this hodgepodge of pillows, rugs, and ceramics that have nothing to do with each other."

"See, you do have something in common with her," Shasta says and winks. I guess she's right. I spend so much time thinking about all the ways Mom and I were completely different, our looks, our grace, it never occurred to me to look at the little things that made us alike.

Shasta rubs her hands together and surveys the table. "Alright, so we've got a crap ton of food, a million different kinds of beverages, an open bar, oh and you're in luck because Stephen got his band back together to play."

"Shut up, Stephen was in a band?" I really shouldn't be surprised he was in a band at some point. He just has that vibe.

"Yup, back in college. They called themselves The Sour Grapes."

I laugh. "You're kidding right?"

She shakes her head. "Nope. The name has always been stupid, but they actually did really well. Won Battle of the Bands every year and a few of their songs played on heavy rotation with the college radio station."

"Awesome. I can't wait to hear them."

Spoiler alert, The Sour Grapes are legit. I don't even know how to describe their sound other than some sort of weird amalgamation of funk punk ska. Like if The Mighty Bostones and Blink 182 had a baby, it would be The Sour Grapes.

I spend a good portion of the evening making rounds with Shasta. She introduces me to their friends I haven't met yet, and chatting with those I have. Kendall has posted up by the open bar, trying to convince the male bartender that he doesn't know how to make a proper Tom Collins, but it's totally obvious he's just trying to get his flirt on.

Mr. and Mrs. Green, who rarely come out due to various health issues, are seated in two of the plush chairs around the fire pit along with the Callahan's. The four of them are roughly the same age, but the Green's look like they're at least ten years older than the Callahan's, who, despite having bad hips and knees act like they're forty instead of sixty.

Caroline is here, but she's glued to her seat at a table in the corner, not once looking up from her phone. To prove how much of a bigger person I can be, I go up to her and slide into the chair next to her.

"Hey Caroline," I say. She continues to click away at her phone and then looks over at me and flashes a fake as hell grin.

"Maddie. So, I hear you're going to be leaving. That's such a bummer."

"Yeah, I'm sure you're real beat up about it. Listen, I just want to say, even though you were a jerk this entire trip, it was nice meeting you, and I don't have any hard feelings."

She's looking at me like I've lost my mind. I don't know, maybe she expected me to be snarky. I just don't have the energy for that.

She arches an eyebrow. "Wish I could say the same." Doesn't take a genius to know she's trying to get a rise out of me. Luckily right at that moment, Caleb calls my name from the buffet table. He's wearing khaki shorts and a red polo shirt and I can't help but laugh because he looks like he's just come off a shift at Target. I get up and leave without saying goodbye and walk over to Caleb. Ten to one Caroline is glaring holes right into my back but I don't really care.

He pulls me into a hug. He smells like Aqua Digio cologne. He is literally killing me right now.

"Man, your sister knows how to throw one hell of a party. And I can't believe she got Stephen and his old band to play."

"You've heard about his band?" I ask.

"Oh yeah. Stephen and his buddies have a habit of reminiscing old times when they hit the bottle too hard. More often than not they do impromptu shows. It's actually pretty hilarious. They can't remember the words half the time and it comes out sounding like that one Pearl Jam song."

"Man, I'm kinda peeved I didn't know any of this. They sound pretty good like this, you know, sober."

"So, Kendall said you're leaving in a few days."

I bite my bottom lip and look away. If I look at him, at those blue saucer eyes I'm going to cave and change my mind and stay forever.

"Yeah. I need to go spend more time with Adelpha before I go back to Oregon. But I'll be back. I mean, I want to visit my sister, and Sarah."

He touches my chin with the tip of his fingers and tilts my face up until I'm looking at him. "Well, I hope you add me to that list." He smiles and leans in, gently kissing me on the lips. It would have been the perfect moment had it not been for stupid Caroline and what she did next.

"Are you freaking kidding me!" Caroline screeches from her table. She pushes up from her chair, knocking it down in the process and marches up to us.

"You know he's my boyfriend, right?" she hisses.

"Jesus, Caroline. I'm not your boyfriend," Caleb says, but Caroline thrusts a palm up to his face, her eyes still glued to mine.

"You must think you're hot shit, coming in here, stealing what doesn't belong to you."

"You're like a broken record, Caroline. For the millionth time, I'm not stealing anything from anyone."

By now the band has stopped playing and everyone in the yard is staring at us. Shasta has come out of the house with a platter in hand. I can feel the heat rising to my cheeks and my fight or flight instincts are telling me to get the hell out of here, but then Caleb reaches down and grabs my hand in his, squeezes, and I'm filled with a heap of Erin-sized confidence.

"I'm just trying to get to know my sister," I say. "But for some lame reason you can't just be okay with that. You seem to think Shasta's going to stop being your sister just because she found out she has another sister and that's really stupid. I just don't get why you can't stop being so lame about this."

Caroline narrows her eyes, and she looks to be two seconds from reenacting that Kristen Wiig scene from *Bridesmaids* before Shasta swoops down from the porch and grabs her.

"What the hell are you doing Caroline?" she asks, holding Caroline by the shoulders at arm's length. Caleb has tucked me into his arms.

Caroline's fists clench, lips purse. She opens her mouth but then snaps it shut. She turns as if to leave but then swivels back around and goes slack in front of Shasta, tears now streaming down her face. "Why'd you have to do that stupid DNA test? Weren't we enough for you?" she cries.

Shasta's face softens. "Oh Caroline, of course you're enough."

She pulls her into a hug, and then then Mr. and Mrs. Callahan join them. I'm suddenly overcome with a strong feeling of awkwardness so without giving too much thought, I slip out of Caleb's arms and make my way for the side gate, and after latching it, take off running down the gravel path to the main road. If there were ever a clear sign that I've overstayed my welcome, it was watching Caroline reach a breaking point in front of their friends and family.

I'm half way down the road when I hear honking behind me followed by a familiar jeep pulling up alongside of me. The window rolls down but I don't look over. I keep my pace, ignoring the fact that these flats were not intended for light jogging.

"Maddie! Maddie will stop?" Caleb hollers from the cab.

"Nope, not gonna do that. Just gonna keep going, thanks."

He accelerates and once a safe distance past me, pulls over to the side of the road and gets out. I'm about to jog past him, but he reaches out, grabs my hand and slows me to a stop.

"Why'd you take off? Where are you going?" he asks.

"Home, Caleb. I'm going home."

"Why are you going home?"

"You saw what I saw. I'm getting in the way," I say. "I'm just going to walk into town and take a bus Adelpha's. I can't wait until tomorrow."

"What about your stuff?" he asks.

"I'll have it shipped or Shasta can burn it for all I care. I just want to leave."

He slides his hand into mine and begins to pull me towards the jeep.

"What are you doing?" I ask.

"I'll drive you."

"Stop. You're not gonna drive me all the way to San Francisco."

"Well, I'm not letting you take the bus."

Chapter Eleven

THE drive to Adelpha's is quiet, just the hum of the radio turned down low, Caleb occasionally singing along. He doesn't try to converse, which is fine because I don't feel much like talking. I need to process everything. I don't know how long it will be before Shasta realizes I've left. 45 minutes into the drive I remember that I don't even have my phone. Would she have called or texted? I'd borrowed Caleb's phone to let Adelpha know I was coming, and afterwards hovered over Shasta's contact but clicked off and handed the phone back to Caleb. She's got enough to deal with right now, i.e Caroline, and I don't want to add to it. I'll just call her once I get to Adelpha's.

Adelpha is sitting outside on the porch swing when we pull up, her small frame wrapped tightly in a blanket. Her smile is warm and inviting and exactly what I needed.

"I'll help you out," Caleb says, unbuckling.

"I'm fully capable of opening a door for myself," I say.

"I know you can, Miss Independent. I'm going to help you anyway because I like you, I'm chivalrous, and I saw the massive blisters on your feet when you took your shoes off."

He pulls open my door and scoops me up, carrying me up the walkway. I'd complain and tell him to put me down if I weren't so tired. Also, my feet hurt like hell. That's what I get for running on gravel in ballet flats. Adelpha drops her blanket and hobbles down the steps to meet us.

"What on earth has happened?"

"I decided to go jogging but I couldn't find my sneakers," I say.

Caleb nods and smiles at Adelpha as he carries me up the steps, into the house and gently lowers me down to the couch in the sitting room.

"I'm going to get the first aid kit." Adelpha pats Caleb gently on the shoulder and heads to the bathroom in the back of the house. Caleb runs a hand through his hair.

"Ok, now that I got you here safely, I'm gonna head out."

"We drove straight here. Don't you want to rest? I'm sure Adelpha wouldn't mind if you crashed here."

"I'd better not. You guys have some talking to do. I'm just gonna crash at my brother's. He's got a place in the city. I'll call Shasta on my way and let her know I got you here safe and sound." He kisses the top of my head and sneaks out as Adelpha returns with the first aid kit.

"Where is the young man going? Why did he leave so abruptly? More importantly, who *is* he?" she asks.

"That's Caleb. Works with Shasta. He's going to his brother's place somewhere in the city."

"Oh. I would have sent him with some food."

She sits next to me on the couch and motions for me to place my feet in her lap.

"Well then, tell me what's transpired. I imagine it must be something dire."

While she goes about cleaning and bandaging my feet, I tell her about Caroline's epic outburst at the party, and my hasty decision to bolt without any of my stuff. When she's finished cleaning my feet and I've told her everything, she closes the first aid kit, sets it down on the table and folds her hands in her lap. I wait for her to say something but she doesn't.

"This is the part where you offer words of wisdom," I say.

"What would you like me to say?"

"Well, do you think I made the right decision?"

"I think you made a decision that was right for you in that moment."

"But not the right one?" I ask.

"Sweetheart, I can't tell you if your decision was right or wrong. My days of telling someone their choices are right or wrong ended long ago. What matters is what you do from this point on. You will have to speak to Shasta. Now, she does already know you are here as she called me moments after you did. She didn't know where you'd gone and was panicked. I told her you were on your way and you'd call her in the morning."

"What do I even say, Grandma? What if she's super pissed that I took off?"

"I'm sure she won't be. Now why don't you head upstairs and get some sleep. I'll make you coffee in the morning."

She's up and heading for her room before I have a chance to say anything else, so I hobble up the stairs and after splashing water on my face and swishing with some mouth wash, I strip out of my dress and collapse into my mom's old bed, pull the covers over my head and pass out.

***

I groan as I hear the clanking of glasses from downstairs. I stick my arm out of the blanket and fumble around the nightstand in search of my phone, then groan again upon remembering I'd left it at Shasta's. I look at the time on the small alarm clock. Quarter after seven. I'm about to pull the blankets back over my head when I hear two voices in the kitchen and catch the swift aroma of coffee.

I swing my legs out of the bed and rummage through Mom's closet until I find some thick socks, sweatpants, and a ratty Depeche Mode sweatshirt before making my way downstairs. Adelpha sits at the round table sipping from her usual mug. I do a double take when I see Shasta next to her. I put up a finger as I walk past them to the coffee pot that I don't recall being here before I left, pour some into a large red mug that declares Hopa! in gold letters. I take a slow sip before turning to face them.

"Your coffee, as promised." Adelpha chuckles.

"It's amazing," I say, slinking into one of the chairs.

"Just because I prefer tea doesn't mean I don't know how to brew a pot of coffee."

I take another drink before looking at Shasta. She doesn't look mad, so to speak, but she does look sort of irritated. I wait for her to go all mother-figure on me.

"So that was some epic Irish goodbye you did last night, Mads," she says. "You didn't even take any of your stuff. What gives?"

"What do you mean? You were there."

"Did you leave because of Caroline?"

I shrug my shoulders. "Partly, I guess. I mean, I was going to leave anyway, she just kinda rushed things along."

"Look, I get that she picked a terrible time to have her little tantrum, but couldn't you have just gone back to my house and waited for me? We could have talked about this."

"There's nothing to talk about, Shasta. The truth is, as much as I have loved getting to know you and your family, I feel like I'm going to be some huge wedge driven in between you and Caroline and I don't like it."

"What? You're not a huge wedge. Caroline will get over her issues."

"And what if she doesn't?" I say, forcing the tears welling up in my eyes to stay put. "What if she never accepts me, never accepts our being sisters and she shuts you out? I can't have you guys acting like Stephen and Paul, who only see each other once a year at the parade. You can promise all you want that *that* won't happen, but you can't guarantee it. I think it's just better if I go home, back to Ashland."

"So what does that mean for us?" Shasta says, swiping the tears on her cheeks. "I just found you. I don't want to lose you."

I shrug my shoulders again, which I realize is a pretty juvenile move, but it's all I've got at the moment. "I don't know."

Shasta purses her lips. "And what about Sarah? She adores you. You're just going to cut her out too?"

"Shasta, I'm not cutting anyone out, I'm saying I don't know how to be a part of your family without causing issues in your family. I just need time. Okay? Can you give me some time and space?"

She pushes away from the table, stands up and finishes her coffee. "I went almost nineteen years. What's a few more in comparison?" And then she leaves the kitchen, grabs her purse from the couch and storms out. I look at Adelpha, which was basically like a punch to the gut because the look on her face is some sort of combination between sadness and disappointment.

"Spit it out, Grandma," I say. "I'm sure you have some sort of opinion on this."

"I'm not going to say anything. I spent too many years telling my opinions to my own daughter and look what that got me? If you think you did what was best, who am I to tell you if you're wrong."

She gets up, places her cup in the sink and comes to a stop behind me. She rests her bony fingers on my shoulders, kisses the top of my head. "It's time for my card game next door. Shasta has brought your belongings. They are by the door in the living room. I'll be back to before lunch."

So now I'm left in the kitchen with just my thoughts, which sucks by the way because right about now I could have used some of the opinions my mother ran far away from. I thought the hardest thing I was ever going to have to go through in my entire life was the death of my mother, but man, was I wrong. I just broke Shasta's heart, Sarah would probably never forgive me, and I don't know if I have the courage to wait around to have "the talk" with Adelpha when she gets back. I already know she's disappointed. What I'm about to do next will just add to that heaping pile of disappointment.

Chapter Twelve

I GET off the bus at the station and scan the parking lot for Rafe, but he's not here. I pull out my phone to check for missed calls or texts from him. There are several texts and missed calls from others, but nothing from Rafe. I wait until the bus driver unloads all of the bags from the compartment, watch as they are picked over by their owners, until only mine remain. When the bus pulls out of the bay, I start to call Rafe but hang up when I hear the familiar squeal of tires and watch as his burnt orange Subaru rounds the corner and cranks to a stop in front of me.

"I am so sorry *mija,* I didn't mean to be late." He jumps out, gives me a quick hug before popping the trunk, scooping up my bags and dumping them in. He smells like turpentine and there are streaks of blue paint smeared across his cheek. I can't help but smile.

"What are you working on that kept you so engaged?" I ask, climbing into the passenger seat and buckling.

"I decided to take on a few interns."

"SOU art students?"

"Nope. High schoolers." He maneuvers out of the bus station, making a left onto a busy Siskiyou Boulevard.

"So this is when you tell me why you booked a last minute bus ticket home."

Getting straight to the point, I see. "I just couldn't stay anymore. Things were getting too complicated."

"Complicated in what way?" he asks.

"The whole being the other sister thing. Caroline had this major breakdown at the Callahan's anniversary party and I just realized I didn't want to get in their way."

"What do you think you'd be getting in their way of?"

"Being sisters."

"*Mija,*" he sighs. "You're just as much Shasta's sister as Caroline is."

"Yeah, I get that *biologically* we're sisters, but they've been sisters for 22 years, Rafe. That's a lot of history to compete with and I am just not the competitive type."

"So what does that mean? You're just never going to see her again? What about Sarah?"

I turn away from him and rest my forehead on the window. People keep mentioning Sarah and it's literally tearing me up inside because I know that as much as I'll miss Shasta, I'll miss Sarah even more. I kept thinking the whole bus ride home that Sarah is going to grow up hating me. When Shasta tells her that I left and she doesn't know if I'll ever come back it's going to totally crush her and that hurts so much to think about.

"How'd your goodbye's go with Adelpha?" Rafe asks.

I bite my lower lip. "I, uh, left her a note. On the kitchen table."

He closes his eyes and swipes his hands across his face. "You left her a note?"

"Yeah. And I know what you're thinking. I did the same exact thing that Mom did. I panicked, okay?"

He turns right onto Morton Avenue and pulls into our driveway at the end of the road. He puts the car in park but leaves it running.

I unbuckle my seatbelt. "Are you not coming inside?"

"I need to go back to the studio for a little bit. Look, I think you should call Adelpha. Don't leave things with just a note. Trust me when I say that for as terribly as your mom and your grandmother got along, she wishes she'd left home in a different manor. Obviously, it's too late for her, but it's not too late for you."

After I haul everything into my room and unpack, I pull my phone out from my bag and see I have three missed calls from Adelpha. When she left for her card game, I waited all of two seconds before packing up and buying a bus ticket home. I'm not usually impulsive, but at the time it just felt like the right thing to do. Maybe not the *right* thing, but just something I *needed* to do. I took an Uber and made it to the bus station all within an hour, and after sending Rafe a text asking him to meet me at the bus station in Ashland, I'd set my phone to *do not disturb*.

Since she doesn't have a cell phone I can't text her, and I'm not ready to call her back, so I make a mental note to do that at some point. I'm still not even sure what I'll say. If she's mad at me and plans to cuss me out in a mix of English and Greek, I don't think I'm in the headspace to handle that.

Along with her missed calls, there are several texts from Caleb, Shasta, and even Kendall. I delete Kendall's texts right away because I never again want to read half the words he called me. What the hell even gives him the right?

Caleb has texted twice, once to ask if I've made it okay, and again to ask when we can FaceTime. My response: *made it. Thx.* He sends three question marks but I ignore them. I know I told him I'd keep in contact with him once I returned, but I don't even know what that contact will mean. Like, will it be just friendly checking-in texts here and there, or more intimate? It's just not even something I can begin to think about right now.

There are a series of texts from Shasta, *you seriously left a note? What the hell is wrong with you? How could you do that to Adelpha?* After the fourth text she had called and left a voice message calling me selfish in a tone I had never even heard her use with Caroline. The worst part is she called a second time and asked how I could leave without saying goodbye to Sarah and how hurt Sarah will be and told me not to bother calling back. After listening I chuck my phone onto the floor, fold my knees up to my chest and sob. I knew I was going to hurt people by leaving, but I guess I figured they'd understand and cut me some slack. I don't think I am being selfish. Coward, yeah, but not selfish.

Here's how the next several weeks play out-I continue to get texts from Caleb and I continue to ignore them. I get texts from Kendall, which I also ignore, and then block his contact. Clearly, he is the *fiercely protective of his people* type and makes it perfectly clear, almost to the point one might say is harassment.

Shasta texted to apologize for how mean she came across in her series of texts and phone calls, and said she didn't mean to tell me not to call back. I should have texted back *it's totally okay, I kinda deserved it* or something like that, or better yet, actually called her back, but instead I send a thumbs up emoji. She hasn't said anything since.

I pick up my shifts at Rare Earth, and even though Michael and Roxy are happy to see me and want to ask questions, they don't, which I appreciate because I'm basically walking around on auto-pilot. I mean, I smile at the customers, I make the small talk, but I'm aware there's probably some vacant expression in my face. Even my father points it out to me during our now bi-weekly dinners. I guess he's decided to stick around town for a little while and direct some local production of *Death of a Salesmen* and he wants to see me more. How convenient. I think he expected me to call him more than the one time I did over the summer, which is comical when you think about it because my whole life, I wanted him to call more, visit more, just show up more, and he acted like I was asking him to donate his liver. Whatever.

I finally summon the courage to call Adelpha back at the end of week two. After several rings, she picks up, huffing and puffing.

"Hello?" she pants.

"Hi Grandma, it's um, me, Maddie. Are you alright?"

"Oh Maddie! Sweetheart, I am fine. I was out in the garden when I heard the phone ring. I didn't want to miss it if it were you calling."

"You know they make these things called mobile phones. You can slip them in to your apron pocket and take them everywhere. Even out to the garden."

She laughs. "Oh how I've missed your wit. How are you my dear? Are you alright? I was so worried"

"I'm okay, Grandma. I'm sorry I didn't call you when I got back to Ashland. I didn't know what to say. I'm also sorry for the way I left, leaving a note. It was a dick move and I'm a jerk."

"Nonsense. You're a lovely young woman."

"You're not mad? It's how mom left and I know how hurt you were by it."

"I am not mad. Of course, I would have preferred to see you off myself, maybe send you with some food, but I understand your need to leave. I was just worried when I didn't hear from you. Had it not been for Rafe calling to let me know you'd arrived, I might have sent a search party."

There's probably some part of her that fears I'll stop talking to her like my mom did and I'm pretty sure that would kill her. That's the last thing I want. After profusely apologizing a thousand more times, I promise to call her once a week, like I'd been doing with Rafe when I was in California. She asks if I've called Shasta and when I tell her no, she encourages me to reach out.

"I don't know, Grandam. I think she's pretty pissed at me. Especially since I sent a thumbs up emoji in response to her last text."

"I'm afraid I don't know what an emoji is, but I do know there is never too late of a time to make amends."

I tell her I'll try to call Shasta, but as we've established, I'm a coward so it'll probably wind up being a pie-crust promise.

***

"Why don't you just call her already?"

It's a slow Saturday at Rare Earth and I'm doing inventory with Roxy. Though she'd been giving me the space I needed, she'd decided it had been long enough. My aura was in need of a change. So I finally gave her the Reader's Digest version of what happened in California.

"I'm not going to call her, Roxy."

She sets her clipboard down on the counter. "Look, sweetheart, I know this Caroline gal sounds like a real piece of work, but is she worth losing your chance at a sister?"

I throw my hands up. "I don't know what you guys aren't getting. Someone here ends up losing a sister. If I continue to get to know Shasta, Caroline will continue to hold a huge fat grudge and stop talking to her, and if I just leave things the way they are, I lose a sister, or the chance at having a sister. It's a lose-lose situation no matter what, but at least with the latter, there's less history to lose."

Roxy shakes her head. "Balderdash."

"Excuse me, but did you actually just say balderdash?"

"Yes, you little Gen Z, believe it or not but back in my day we said balderdash instead of...whatever your generation says. Honey, look, I know you think you're doing the right thing here, but I can see it all over your face that you aren't so sure."

I sigh, because at this point, it's the only thing I can do. I don't know how many different ways I've told everyone that I just don't want the drama, and they all end up saying variations of the same thing: there's no such thing as living a life void of drama; family dynamics are complicated but with time and a little effort are worth it.

"Roxy's totally right!" Erin dumps an armful of dresses onto the counter. She's been coming down more often on the weekends and hangs out with me in the shop. I would be lying if I didn't say it basically feels like she's babysitting me.

"Go on, tell me more about how right I am," Roxie says, winking at Erin.

Erin folds the dresses and slides them across the counter to Roxie who makes a check-mark on the paper attached to her clip-board. "Ok so I know at first I was super skeptical about Shasta, but Mads, she seems like a really cool, genuine person. Plus, she has amazing taste in music and clothes. I mean, she repurposes old band t-shirts! That's awesome. Are you sure you want to give that up?"

"I'm not giving it up, not all the way. I'm just taking a step back to see what I really want from this relationship." I take the folded dresses from Roxie and set them on a table.

"OMG you just talked about her like she was your boyfriend rather than your sister. Look, Caroline is a bitch, but she doesn't have the only claim to Shasta, and I know you've spent your whole life an only child, but I've also seen the way you envy my relationship with Maris. Don't you remember when we were little and you always used to say you wished you had a sister?"

I nod. I'd thought of Erin as a sister, and Leonard as my brother. My mom used to say that your family doesn't have to be the one you're born into, but the one you choose and I always felt part of both their families. As great a feeling as that was, I couldn't help saying, "at least you have a sibling" whenever either would be fighting with one of their siblings.

As if she were reading my mind, Erin cocks her head to the side and smiles. "You know I've always thought of you as a sister, Maris too. And my dad calls you his third child. But still, you have a real blood related sister and I think you're going to regret it if you decide to cut her out."

"You should listen to your friend," Roxie says.

I groan. "Let's talk about something else, okay?"

Erin slides a coy grin across her face. "Okay, tell me about your boyfriend."

"What's this about a boyfriend?" Roxie asks.

I feel myself blushing. "He's not my boyfriend."

"Yeah but you want him to be," Erin says, jacking her eyebrows up and down. I kick her under the table when she opens her mouth because I know she's seconds away from singing that stupid kissing song.

"Ouch!" she shrieks, then laughs.

"You're such a child."

"Fine. I won't sing the song. But really, tell me about Caleb."

"There's not much to tell," I say.

"What do you mean? You spent a lot of time with him over the summer and I could tell by the way you talked about him every time I called that you like him. Kinda sounds like he likes you too."

I shrug. "I mean, yeah I really like him and we even kissed but-"

"Wait what?!" Erin interjects, eyes widening to the size of two full moons. "Did you say you kissed? Why the hell didn't you just lead with that?"

"Because it was just a kiss, and it can only ever be a just kiss. He and Caroline have too much history and besides, he lives in California and I live here."

"First of all, the whole he and Caroline and too much history stuff is bull crap. They dated in the past. They aren't dating now and the 'whole don't date my sisters' exes' doesn't apply because she's not actually your sister. Secondly, who cares if he lives in California. You could have a long-distance thing, like me and Leonard."

I shake my head. "It's different. You're in Eugene, Leonard is in Corvallis. Those towns aren't that far away. Caleb and I are in two completely different States. Also, if we started dating, I'd want to go down there and visit him but he works with Shasta and Stephen so I'd see them and that defeats the whole purpose of my leaving. Also, I kinda haven't talked to him since I've been back."

"You're kidding. You've been home for weeks! Why have you been ghosting him too?" she asks.

I roll my head back and groan. "I don't know! Because I'm an idiot? I texted him the day after I got home, but that's it. He's sent like five texts asking why I've been ignoring him and I can't bring myself to respond."

She shakes her head at me. "Maddie, I love you but you're utterly ridiculous."

I spend the rest of the weekend thinking about Caleb. Erin's right. I am being ridiculous. So when she heads back up to school, I muster up the courage to FaceTime him. When he picks up, he's got sweat dripping down his brow.

"Well if it isn't my old pal Ashland. Wondered when I was going to hear from you."

"You're sweating like a pig. Did I catch you at a wrong time?" I ask.

"Nah, just moving wine barrels with my dad."

"I can call back if you're busy."

"This is a fine time," he says. "I can take a break. What's up?"

I can't tell by his tone if he's mad at me for ghosting him. He's smiling and genuinely looks happy to hear from me. Maybe he's just not the type to hold a grudge. I mean, he's still friends with Caroline and she's probably been a bitch to him on more than a few occasions.

"Well, I just wanted to, um.."

"To what?" he interjects. "See my beautiful face?"

"Obviously. No I uh,"

He waves a hand around in a "spit it out" motion. "You're not going to make this easy for me, are you?" I ask.

He laughs and shakes his head. "Not in the slightest."

"OK fine. I'm sorry. I should have called you back sooner."

"Yes, you should have. Go on," he says.

"And I won't ignore you anymore."

He smiles and then the screen pauses. "Caleb? Are you there?"

My phone vibrates and I see it's a text from Caleb: *hi there.* I laugh and text him back: *hi there yourself.* The screen un-pauses and he smiles. I want to kiss his freaking face so much.

"If I call you tonight, are you going to answer?"

"Yes. I'm going to answer."

"Okay. I gotta get back to work."

"Okay."

I'm about to slide my phone into my pocket when it rings. It's Caleb FaceTiming. I swipe to answer.

"Just checking," he says.

"You're a punk. I'll talk to you later."

And I do. He calls as I'm closing up the store and we talk on my walk home. We talk while I heat up some dinner and continue talking for most of the night. The conversation is all over the place, bouncing from one topic to the next. It's almost like picking up where we'd left off the day we ran into one another in the park in Calistoga. He fills me in a little on how Shasta and the rest of the family have been. I try not to wince when he tells me Shasta hasn't been her normal peppy self. I know it's because of me. I'm slightly shocked to hear Caroline has been working at making amends for the whole party blow-out, and mending her relationship with Shasta, which is good, I guess. I mean, it's the whole reason I left right? So I should be feeling happy about it. Instead, if I'm being honest, it just makes me sad, and probably a little jealous. Why *should* Caroline have the only claim at being Shasta's sister? Don't I deserve a bit of that too? Whatever. I'd made my choice so I'm going to be happy with this bit of news, even if I really just want to cry.

Chapter Thirteen

IT'S November, and I still haven't contacted Shasta. Last month she'd sent a few texts begging me to talk to her, but I didn't respond. Why didn't I respond, one might ask? Well, because I'm an idiot. I know eventually she'll stop texting because there's only so long a person can attempt to maintain a relationship before their give-a-crap meter runs out. I wouldn't even blame her. Besides, what would I say at this point? It's not for lack of trying. I mean, I did draft several texts with the intention of sending, but I just couldn't get my stupid finger to hit send.

To keep myself occupied, I've been throwing myself into work, picking up any extra hours at Rare Earth. I think Roxy would rather I focus on figuring out my life plan, but I can tell she appreciates all the free time she's been getting by my working more. She may love the store, but I also know she loves traveling with Michael in their RV. I mean, they leave their nephew, Alex, in charge when they are gone, but he's kind of a tool, always sitting in the office on his computer, doesn't understand how to do inventory properly, and has zero interest in actually running the business.

Today, for example, Alex decided he'd rather check out the new comic book supply at More Fun Comics, so I'm by myself, and it's a slow Wednesday afternoon. Which is fine. Weekends are bustling with tourists and it can be hectic, so I appreciate the mid-week lull.

I'm sorting a rack of bohemian dresses by color when I hear the bell on the door chime. "Hi, welcome to Rare Earth, let me know if I can help you find anything," I call out without turning to look at the door.

"Like this store would ever have anything I'd be caught dead in." I freeze. There's no freaking way. I'd recognize that catty voice anywhere. I hang up the dress I'd been holding and slowly turn towards the door and sure enough, Caroline Callahan is standing there, in her designer jeans and pea coat that looks like it costs more than I've ever made here, scanning every corner of the store with a look of disgust. *What in the actual fuck is she even doing here?*

"Hey Caroline," I say. "Did you make a wrong turn somewhere?"

She waits before she responds, almost like she's thinking carefully about what words she wants to say so she doesn't spew vomit, which is her usual M.O. Her face softens and she drops her arms to her side as she approaches me. On instinct, I take several steps back until I'm almost falling into the clothes rack.

"What are you doing?" I ask, throwing my hands up to guard my face.

"Relax. I'm not going to hit you. I just got my nails done. I came to apologize." She all but chokes on that last word.

"I'm sorry, I must not have heard you correctly. You what now?"

She rolls her eyes and groans. "You heard me. I came to say sorry. I was a wicked bitch at my sister's...*our* sister's party. I never should have lashed out like that, and I never should have treated you the way I did."

Well that was unexpected. "You know you didn't have to drive all the way up here to apologize. They make these things called cell phones. You could have just called."

She snorts. "Get real. Would you have actually answered?"

I shrug. "Probably not. And I'd probably have deleted your text before reading it."

"Which is why I drove up here. I've never been to Ashland. This is um, quite the eclectic little town."

I nod. "People tend to like it."

"Look, I really am sorry. I was jealous. For 22 years it was just me and Shasta and even though I've always been a bitch, she's been the only one to see through that and love me, I mean, besides my parents, although at the moment I'm not even sure they do. Shasta really misses you. A lot. She's all mopey, always checking her phone in case you text or call, and don't even get me started on Sarah. She keeps asking why you left and if you're coming back."

"She does?" I ask.

"Of course. You're the cool aunt." She says this with absolutely no hint of sarcasm.

"When Shasta told us she has a biological sister and she wanted to meet you, I got scared, and then felt threatened because you turned out to be this awesome person, and I've never been very good at sharing. Even when something isn't mine anymore, i.e. Caleb, I'm not good at sharing. And I know it sounds stupid, but I thought that since you guys share actual DNA, she'd like you more than me. Please don't shut them out because of me. Shasta is your sister just as much as she is mine and I promise to reign in my crazy jealousy. She needs you, and I think you need her too."

I stand there with my mouth open, like a frog waiting for a fly. I should be happy, right? She's here apologizing and it sounds like a genuine apology, but this is also Caroline we're talking about and she's screwed me over before. Who's to say she's not just messing with me again? What if Shasta's actually waiting in the car outside and I follow Caroline out and she tosses a slushie at me from the window?

I shake my head. "Here's the thing, Caroline, you seem like you mean what you say, and I really, really want to believe you, but I also don't want to be gullible."

She sighs, whips out her phone, sends a quick text and then says, "Kay I get it. Maybe you'll believe me if he confirms it."

The door opens and Caleb walks in holding a bouquet of dahlias. He's wearing dark blue jeans, a flannel jacket, and a black beanie, which is so stereotypically Oregon-hipster but he pulls it off. He's got his usual crooked grin spread across his face and I can't think of anything witty to say so instead I basically push past Caroline, run towards him and jump into his arms. It's a move so uncharacteristic of me. We'd been FaceTiming every few days, but I didn't actually think I'd see him in person any time soon. After a quick spin, he sets me down and gently kisses my lips. I almost forget Caroline is there until she lets out a fake gag.

"It's gonna take a long time to get used to that," she says.

Caleb hands me the flowers and tucks a loose strand of hair behind my ear. "Caroline said you might need some convincing so she asked me to tag along."

I shrug my shoulders and grin. "I mean...can you blame me?"

He looks at her and then back at me, laughs. "Given your past experience, no not really. Trust me though, after driving with her for several hours listening to her yammer about her desire to change, she's being genuine. She really does mean it."

"What if it's too late? I haven't been responding to any of Shasta's texts. What if I've hurt her too badly?"

Caroline shakes her head in protest. "Trust me, with the way she's been moping, there's no freaking way she wouldn't be excited to hear from you. Also, Shasta like never holds grudges. It's kind of annoying."

I've been trying to justify my decision to run from the chance to have a sister, believing that I was doing the best thing, not just for me, but for everyone. In truth, I was just thinking of myself, my discomfort with the drama, my inability to handle confrontation without a buffer. I'd wanted for so long to feel there was some part of me that was just like my mom and since I didn't get her looks, I figured if I just ran away exactly as she did, I'd feel a connection. I'd be all "hey mom look, we're both cowards" and it would somehow make me feel good. Instead, it just showed what kind of a huge idiot I was. I had the courage to go all the way to California to meet a grandmother I didn't know, and then a sister I didn't know, but I lacked the courage to fight for that sister. So go figure it would take Caroline humbling herself before me, an act I didn't even know she was capable of doing what with her Mean Girl attitude, to drive home my idiocy.

I spend the rest of the day with Caroline and Caleb, taking them around Ashland, and then back to my place for one of Rafe's famous dinners, and it's nice to see what Caroline is actually like when she's not actively trying to tear me down. She's still kind of vapid and self-centered, but there's also a weird sort of tenderness to her where I can easily start to see why Shasta loves being her sister. When she looks at me, it's no longer with irritation and hate but instead with her version of kindness. It's weird, but at the same time awesome, mainly because once you get past her bullshit, she really does remind me of Erin, like an insane amount. I think I'll like having her as a quasi-sister.

After Caroline and Caleb leave, I muster up the courage call Shasta. Once she takes a second to express her confusion and disbelief at the unselfishness of Caroline, she bawls her eyes out when I apologize for being an idiot.

"Oh Maddie, you weren't being an idiot. I mean, you were a little, but I get it. You were scared. I was scared to reach out to you, but I'm glad I did. And I'm glad you want to be sisters. I miss you, kiddo."

"I really miss you too, Shasta. And I miss Stephen, and Kendall, when he's not cussing at me, and I miss Sarah like a crazy unbelievable amount."

At the mention of Sarah, a switch flips and I start to bawl, and then we're both bawling, like two big freaking babies. I don't think I've ever cried like this in all my life, well, except for maybe when my mom told me she was dying. At one point, Rafe even pokes his head into my room to check on me and then walks away laughing after I manage to articulate I'm making up with Shasta.

Here's the thing I realized once we'd cried our eyes dry. Everything Erin said about me being envious of her and Maris was totally true. I mean, it's probably why any chance I got to spent at their house, listening to their fights, observing them like some anthropology researcher or something, I took it. Somewhere deep down inside was a desire to be part of a siblinghood, a *sisterhood*. As weird as it might sound, but because of the lifestyle in which I was raised, I think I've always had that longing because the Universe was going to bring Shasta and I together. Do I wish it would have been when Mom was alive? Yeah, sure. Of course. I think that she could have used the healing too.

I'll never know why Mom felt she couldn't just be honest about who she was when she was younger, or get to ask her what made her feel she was ready to be a mom when I was born. I'm not going to dwell on it, or let myself be too angry about it, because the Callie I got to know for eighteen years, I believe, has always been the best version of her. The version she was meant to be, and the Fates, destiny, or some other higher power must have figured once she was gone, I was going to need someone to connect with, someone to belong to, and who better than this woman who looks exactly like her?

March 15 2022

Hey Grandma,

Day one of "the three sisters' spring break" road trip is complete and already I think I've made a huge mistake. Caroline is a terrible driver and Shasta insists on stopping at every roadside attraction, and the hotel we're at doesn't have Wi-Fi. If I don't make it to your house for Easter, you'll know why. Just kidding. We're having a great time. The Grand Canyon is breathtaking. Can't wait to see you at the end of the trip!

Love,

Maddie.

Acknowledgements

My favorite part of any book I read, even if I didn't end up particularly enjoying it, has always been the Acknowledgements page. Often times I will read it first because it gives me a small sense of who the author is before I dive into the story they've created. It's silly really, because unless I happen to know the author, I'm not going to know a single person they are thanking, but I can't help but read each name and mentally give them a high five for helping the author live out their dream.

So, a million thanks to the members of my family. Often times we go months without conversing, but when we do, you ask if I'm still writing and that means the world.

The Ernie to my Bert-Rachel Petetit. Thank you for happily accepting long text messages of manuscript and telling me what was hot garbage.

Sarah Higgins, who was my writing partner earlier on in my life. I probably would have given up long ago if not for you.

And to Jerkface, for reading my stuff even though there aren't goblins, warlocks, or dragons.

About the Author

Angela L Keith lives and writes in Salem, Oregon. When not schlepping around her two kids and chunky Corgi, she loves to read, practice yoga, and she prefers salty chips to chocolate cake because she's a weirdo.

www.ingramcontent.com/pod-product-compliance
Lightning Source LLC
Chambersburg PA
CBHW050405110726
47899CB00008B/2656